EVEN BEFORE THEY REACHED THE KNOLL, THERE
CAME A TERRIFIC BLAST!

The Message in the Hollow Oak

The Message in the Hollow Oak

BY CAROLYN KEENE

NEW YORK

Grosset & Dunlap

PUBLISHERS

CONTENTS

Contents

CHAPTER I

A Winning Title

"Carson Drew, Attorney at Law . . . Private."

Nancy frowned as she regarded the neatly-lettered sign on the door of her father's inner office. Her pretty face was flushed, and her blue eyes sparkled with excitement. She had such wonderful news to relate, yet it seemed that the door would never open. Conferences took entirely too long!

"It's hard to wait," she told Mr. Drew's efficient secretary.

"I'd tell your father you are here, but he especially requested me not to disturb him."

"Oh, I shouldn't want to interrupt him," Nancy said hastily. "I imagine the conference is very important, or it wouldn't take so long."

"Your father is conferring with Marcus Taylor, I believe."

Nancy looked up with interest.

"Not the builder who holds such extensive lumber interests in the North?"

"Yes, I believe that is the man. At any rate, I know Mr. Taylor is bringing suit against a Canadian company, for I worked on some of the papers in the case this morning."

"I've heard a great deal about him," Nancy remarked. "I should like to meet him very much."

She lowered her voice just then, for the inside office door had opened. Carson Drew and a ruddy-cheeked individual of about fifty emerged. The latter wore loose fitting garments, and walked along with the easy glide of one who has spent the greater part of his life in the out-of-doors.

"Well, Nancy, this is indeed a pleasant surprise," the lawyer smiled at his daughter, turning to present his companion to her. "Nancy, this is Mr. Taylor."

"Chip off the old block, I'll warrant," the lumberman chuckled. "I've heard it said she could run you out of business, Mr. Drew, if she was of a mind to hang up her shingle!"

Nancy laughed at the implied compliment, and then changed the subject.

"I am taking a vacation from mysteries just now, Mr. Taylor. I'm interested in broadcasting at present."

"Broadcasting?" her father inquired.

"Oh, Dad, that's what I came here to tell

you!" Nancy could not withhold her news another instant. "I've won first prize in a radio contest!"

"I didn't even know that you had entered one," Carson Drew returned in surprise.

"I did it a short while ago on the spur of the moment, and then forgot all about it until the letter came today. You see, the Velvet Company offered a prize to the person who suggested the best mystery title for a continued story written by Ann Chapelle. I listened to each broadcast because the tale was so interesting. Just for the fun of it I sent in a title, never expecting to win even a small prize. I was astonished when the letter and deed arrived."

"Deed?" her father inquired alertly.

"Yes. The Velvet Company also sent me a map so that I might locate the land."

"Do you mean to tell me you've been awarded a piece of real estate, Nancy?"

"Yes, and I'm so excited about it. I've never owned a tract of land before."

"Where is this property?" her father demanded suspiciously. "Some place down in Florida, buried two feet under water?"

Nancy took the deed from her pocket and thrust it into Mr. Drew's hand.

"Don't look so glum, Father," she said. "It's in Canada, and I'm sure it must be worth something."

"Worth the taxes on it," Carson Drew responded dryly. He glanced briefly at the paper, then handed it over to his companion. "You are familiar with Canadian land, Mr. Taylor. Can you tell us anything about this place?"

"The property seems to be located in the vicinity of Lake Wellington," the lumberman informed the two. "I frequently spend my summers there."

"Then is it a nice place?" Nancy asked.

"Very pleasant in summer, but cold as Greenland in winter. The land itself is unimproved, valued principally for its timber and mineral rights. But if your property should happen to be located near the lake, it might be used as a summer resort or a fishing camp."

"I fear it won't be worth anything," Nancy admitted, a trifle crestfallen.

"The best way to find out is to go there," Carson Drew declared cheerfully.

"There won't be much chance of that, I fear, from what Mr. Taylor says. It's too great a distance," she sighed.

"It isn't that far away," Marcus Taylor smiled. "Wild country, of course, but not a great distance from a railroad."

"Why not go up there and look over the property?" Mr. Drew suggested.

Nancy stared in amazed delight.

"Do you really mean that, Father?"

"Yes, if you can find some older person to accompany you. I'll be out of town for a week or so on business. That would be an excellent time for you to make the trip."

"Mr. Taylor, you're not going to Lake Wellington, are you?" Nancy asked eagerly.

The lumberman shook his head regretfully.

"I wish I could get away for a few weeks, I'm so homesick for the smell of pine air. Can't make it, though, until my lawsuit is wiped off the slate. But I know a woman who is leaving for the place in a few days!"

"Would she take me with her, do you think?" Nancy asked hopefully.

"She would if I were to ask her. We're old friends. Why, Mrs. Taylor and I have stayed at Mrs. Donnelly's boarding house every summer we've spent in the North. She's a motherly soul and would take right good care of you."

"Where is she now?" Carson Drew questioned.

"She's expected in River Heights within a few days, I understand. She has been visiting a sister living near by, but is coming here. She'll be returning to Canada shortly to open up her boarding house for the summer."

"May I go with her, Father?" Nancy asked.

"If she's willing to take you along, I see no reason why you should not make the trip. I'll speak to her at the very first opportunity."

"I wish Bess Marvin and George Fayne could go with me, too," Nancy went on, thinking aloud. "What a lark that would be!"

Few persons guessed that George and Bess were girl cousins, so unlike were they in appearance and disposition. Bess was pretty, lady-like and sedate. She took pride in her person, and gave particular care to her luxurious locks. George had cropped her straight dark hair as short as the style would permit, and combed and brushed it as infrequently as possible. It was her desire to be just as boyish looking as she could, and carried out her name as much as she dared.

"What would you think of Mrs. Donnelly chaperoning the girls and myself?" Nancy repeated.

"I'd feel sorry for the poor woman!" her father teased. "But all joking aside, I think it's splendid that you have won the tract of land, and I hope it turns out to be valuable."

Nancy took leave of the lumberman. Then, with the precious deed in her purse she hurried away to show it to her chums, George and Bess. She hoped that they would be able to accompany her North, for with them in the party the trip would be certain to develop into a splendid adventure.

She tripped along with a light step, so engrossed in building beautiful air castles that she hardly noticed where she was going. The loud toot of an automobile horn sounded in her ears. Looking around, she realized that she was at the busy intersection across from the National Bank.

As she waited for a signal, that she might be able to cross the street, she saw an elderly lady coming toward her, bent low beneath the weight of a heavy suitcase. Impulsively Nancy rushed to the stranger's aid.

"You shouldn't carry such a big load," the girl chided gently. "Please let me help you."

With a tired sigh the white-haired woman relinquished her burden.

"I am almost worn out," she admitted, smiling at Nancy. "You see, I expected a man to meet me here but he failed to keep the appointment. Maybe you've seen him—he'd be in a dark red car."

Nancy shook her head.

"I haven't, but he may be along any minute now. Have you far to go?"

"Several blocks," she replied. "However, I must stop at a bank to change a twenty-dollar bill."

"The National Bank is just across the street," Nancy indicated. "If you like, I'll stay here with the suitcase while you do your errand."

"That's very kind of you, I'm sure. It will take me only five minutes."

The woman cautiously made her way across

the street, and disappeared into the bank. Ten minutes passed, and still she did not return. Nancy grew a trifle impatient as she waited at the curb with the heavy grip.

"It would be a good joke on me if she shouldn't come back," the girl thought uneasily. "I'm always getting into trouble doing impulsive things."

At that moment a dark red automobile drew up to the curb. The driver, a dapper man in his late thirties, hailed Nancy.

"I'll relieve you of that suitcase, young lady," he cried.

Nancy regarded him suspiciously.

"I am keeping it for an elderly woman who is in the bank."

"Sure, I know," he smiled disarmingly. "She's my grandmother."

"Then you're the man in the red car who was supposed to meet her?"

"That's right. I was held up in a traffic jam."

The man stepped from the machine, and before Nancy could protest took the suitcase and placed it in the rear luggage compartment.

"I'll run over to the bank and tell her you are waiting," Nancy offered.

She hurried across the street. Entering the building, she was greatly relieved to meet the elderly woman just inside the doorway.

"Your grandson is waiting for you," Nancy

explained. "He drove up in the car and I left the suitcase with him."

"But I have no grandson."

Nancy was bewildered.

"This man drove up in a dark red car, and said you were his grandmother. I hope I have made no mistake——"

In panic she rushed to the street. Her worst fears were confirmed. The man in the red car had vanished!

CHAPTER II

THE THEFT

"HE's gone!"

Nancy's heart sank as she realized how easily she had been misled by the man in the red car. She felt responsible for the theft of the suitcase since it had been left in her care.

"Oh, it was all my fault," she declared self-accusingly. "Was the bag very valuable?"

"Yes, it contained some papers which I can't afford to lose," the woman returned, trying to hide her distress. "Perhaps the suitcase hasn't been stolen after all. The driver may actually have been my friend."

As they hastened across the street, Nancy described the stranger's appearance.

"He was of early middle age and well dressed, though somewhat flashily so. His hair was light, his eyes sharp and piercing."

"Then it couldn't have been the one who was to meet me, for his hair is dark. Oh, I'm afraid you are right. The bag has been stolen. What shall I do?"

"We must notify the police."

Nancy had caught a glimpse of an officer at

the next corner, and hurriedly acquainted him
with the details of the daring theft. He
glanced sharply at Nancy and questioned her
companion further.

"Where did you meet this girl? Did you
mention to her that the bag contained valu-
ables?"

"I met her on the street, and she offered to
help me carry the suitcase. I don't believe I
told her the bag was valuable until after it had
disappeared."

"If you have any doubt as to my integrity
you might inquire of almost anyone here in
River Heights," Nancy said proudly. "My
father, Carson Drew, is well known in the
city."

"You're Carson Drew's daughter?" the officer demanded incredulously.

"Yes, I am."

"Then I'll vouch for her honesty, Ma'am."

"I am Mrs. Donnelly from Canada," the
woman informed the policeman. "I never
doubted this young lady's honesty, for I pride
myself upon being a good judge of character.
The man in the red car stole the bag."

Nancy was amazed when she learned the
identity of the woman whom she had befriended, though she did not at that moment
comment upon the fact.

"Did you take the license number of the
car?" the policeman asked her.

Nancy was forced to admit that she had failed to do so. However, she gave a detailed description of the man as well as his machine.

"I'll call headquarters right away," the officer promised. "The cruiser may be able to pick him up."

"I am afraid the bag is gone," Mrs. Donnelly said disconsolately, after the officer had left to find a telephone. "I don't know what I shall do unless I get it back, for it contains my return ticket to Canada."

Nancy made a sudden decision.

"My roadster is parked on a lot only a block from here. I'll get it and pursue the thief myself!"

Mrs. Donnelly clutched the girl's arm nervously.

"Oh, no, you mustn't do that! It would be too dangerous!"

"I'll take no unnecessary risks. That man has a good start, and if we wait until his description has been broadcast by the police it may be too late for us to overtake him."

"Then see if you can trace the car," Mrs. Donnelly urged gratefully, "but be careful. I'll wait in the bank until you return."

Nancy ran to the nearby parking lot, and a moment later had the roadster in motion. She was not very confident that she could overtake the red car; yet it seemed reasonable to her to believe that the thief would take the main boulevard which led to the outskirts of River Heights.

"He'll try to get out of town as quickly as possible," she thought. "If luck should favor me, I may catch him."

Luck had always favored Nancy, yet those who knew her well maintained that good fortune attended her largely because of her own efforts. Left motherless at an early age, the girl developed considerable resourcefulness and courage. Her mind was unusually keen, she had warm sympathy for those in trouble, and her interest in mysteries had earned her an enviable reputation as a detective. Her father, a noted criminal lawyer, was very proud of her ability, and enjoyed discussing unusual phases of his work with her. Often she helped him clear up puzzling points.

Nancy's first "case," related in the initial volume of this series, "The Secret of the Old Clock," brought her into conflict with an arrogant family, the Tophams. Later a queer bungalow, a delightful old ranch, a mysterious inn, and even a strange old farm provided background for her sleuthing prowess.

Her most recent adventure, recounted in "The Clue of the Broken Locket," resulted in the happy reunion of a war veteran with his sister, and established the bewildering identity of adopted twin babies.

Bess Marvin and George Fayne, who lived

only a few blocks apart, usually shared in Nancy's good times. Nothing piqued the cousins more than to be excluded from a mystery.

"I wonder what they'll say when I tell them about my meeting Mrs. Donnelly under such queer circumstances," Nancy reflected, skillfully guiding her roadster through heavy traffic. "Unless I can manage to overtake that thief, I'll feel a little ashamed to tell the story. After all, I should have been more alert. It was stupid of me to have allowed him to get away with the suitcase!"

She had not liked the stranger's appearance; in fact, she had been reluctant to hand over to him the suitcase. But because he had driven up in a red car, she had accepted his word that he was a grandson of Mrs. Donnelly.

As she reached the less congested part of the city, Nancy put on more speed, driving a little faster than the law allowed.

"If I'm arrested, I'll have a good reason for it, at least," she told herself.

She watched closely for the red car, peering up the various side streets as she passed them, but there was no sign of the thief. She drove several miles beyond the outskirts of the city, and after inquiring at a number of filling stations, reluctantly turned back, convinced that she had taken the wrong road.

"Poor Mrs. Donnelly," the girl thought. "I hate to tell her that I have failed."

She was approaching a traffic light, and accordingly slowed down. Several other automobiles were already waiting for the signal to change. This it did just as Nancy came to a standstill. At that instant she caught a glimpse of a red car crossing the intersection!

The Drew girl accelerated the motor, and began the pursuit. Taking the driver of the other car by surprise, she succeeded in drawing abreast of his machine. One glance at his face told her she had made no mistake. He was the man who had stolen the suitcase!

As she tooted her horn, the culprit gave her a panic-stricken look, and speeded up. A less courageous driver might have abandoned the chase, but Nancy did not intend to be outdistanced. Again she overtook the car.

"Stop!" she cried.

The fellow paid no attention to her command, so his pursuer tooted her horn to attract the attention of passing motorists. Suddenly with a sharp twist of the wheel she crossed directly in front of the red car, blocking its path. Either the thief would have to stop, or else cause a crash.

For one terrifying moment Nancy thought the fellow intended to keep on. Suddenly the brakes screeched on the pavement, and his machine came to a quivering halt. The driver sprang out and started to run.

"Stop him!" Nancy cried out. "Don't let him escape!"

By this time a number of automobiles had halted, and pedestrians were gathering. Two men overtook the thief, dragging him back to the car.

"He stole an old lady's suitcase," Nancy cried. "The police are after him."

"It's a lie," the man snarled, struggling to free himself.

Nancy ran to the back of the red car, raising the lid of the luggage compartment. Triumphantly she displayed Mrs. Donnelly's property.

"The bag is mine," the thief insisted angrily. "This silly girl has mistaken me for another person."

However, the crowd seemed inclined to believe Nancy's story. The two pedestrians maintained a firm hold upon the thief until he was turned over to police officers.

"If you are innocent it will be an easy matter for you to prove it at headquarters," Nancy assured the prisoner as he was taken away. "The suitcase will be opened there in the presence of Mrs. Donnelly."

"You'll pay for this outrage!" the man snapped.

Nancy followed the police in her own

roadster, pausing only long enough to pick up Mrs. Donnelly, who was waiting in the lobby of the National Bank.

"Goodness me, I don't see how you managed to overtake that man so quickly," the elderly lady praised. "I never expected to see the bag again. Oh, I can't thank you enough!"

At the station house Mrs. Donnelly promptly identified her suitcase, then confronted the prisoner. She stiffened slightly as she saw him.

"Tom Stripe!" she cried. "I've always known you were mean and low-down, but I never thought you'd stoop to become a common thief!"

"You know this man?" Nancy asked in amazement.

"Know him? Of course I do. He made trouble between another family and my own. Of late he's held a grudge against me because of a valuable timber tract I hold near Wellington Lake."

"We'll see that he doesn't bother you for some time at least," an officer promised. "A few weeks in jail will do him good."

Tom Stripe was led away, muttering to himself. Nancy could not understand what he was saying, but she did not doubt but that he was threatening either Mrs. Donnelly or herself.

"I wish you would accept a reward for recovering my suitcase," the Canadian woman urged the Drew girl as the two left the police station together.

"Oh, I couldn't do that. I'm as relieved as you are to get the bag again because I felt responsible for its loss. If you'll tell me where you are staying, I'll take you there in my roadster."

Mrs. Donnelly hesitated a moment.

"I wrote to some friends I was coming. I am not certain now they are expecting me, for they did not meet me."

"I'll be glad to take you wherever you wish to go."

"Then I guess I'll head for the Taylor house, anyway. Marcus Taylor and his wife are old friends of mine. I've known Marcus nearly thirty years—ever since he was a lumberjack."

"I met Mr. Taylor for the first time today," Nancy said. "For years the old homestead has been closed, so the family isn't very well known in River Heights."

"Marcus spends most of his time in the North. He's a fine man and a loyal friend."

"He spoke very highly of you."

Mrs. Donnelly looked surprised as well as pleased.

"Did he say anything about expecting me to visit here?"

"Why, I believe he said you intended to visit your sister, and come to River Heights later."

"That's what I wrote in my first letter. Later I received word from my sister that she wouldn't be at home for several days, so I wrote Marcus again, asking that his son meet me. I hope he got the letter."

"No doubt he did. I shouldn't worry about it. I know where the Taylor house is, so I'll drive you there."

A few minutes later Nancy parked her car in front of a rambling, old-fashioned homestead. She carried the heavy suitcase up the walk and set it down on the porch. Anxiously Mrs. Donnelly rang the bell.

"I do hope they're at home," she said nervously.

Marcus Taylor appeared at the door. From the expression on his face it was obvious that he was not looking for Mrs. Donnelly. Nevertheless, he greeted her heartily and insisted that Nancy also come in for a few minutes.

"Mrs. Taylor is somewhere about the place," he said cordially, taking the woman's suitcase. "I'll call her."

"I can tell you weren't looking for me," Mrs. Donnelly declared uneasily. "Didn't you get a letter I mailed from Chicago?"

"It must have miscarried," Marcus Taylor returned, "but that doesn't make a bit of difference. We always have an extra room for you. I've been wanting to see you today anyway, because I have a favor to ask of you."

"What is it?" Mrs. Donnelly smiled.

Marcus Taylor winked slyly at Nancy.

"When you return to Wellington Lake, I want you to chaperon a young lady friend of mine."

"I'll be glad to do that, Marcus, but I hope she isn't one of these silly modern creatures who can't do a thing for themselves."

"You should be a judge of that, because you've already met her!"

Mrs. Donnelly stared at Nancy.

"Surely he doesn't mean you!" she gasped.

"I'm afraid he does," Nancy laughed. "It was a strange coincidence, our meeting."

"A fortunate one for me, my dear. I'll be mighty glad to take you with me back to Wellington Lake. But tell me, what brings you to such an isolated spot?"

Nancy explained about the prize contest, and impulsively offered the deed for Mrs. Donnelly's inspection. To the girl's satisfaction, the woman put on her spectacles and studied the paper carefully.

"Well, what do you think of it?" Marcus Taylor demanded, as she finally returned the document to Nancy. "You're a clever trader when it comes to a land deal, Mrs. Donnelly. If you would say the property is valueless it might save the girl a hard trip."

Mrs. Donnelly hesitated a long while before offering her opinion.

"I don't like to build up false hopes, for one really can't be sure of a thing."

"I wish you would give me your honest opinion," Nancy urged. "After all, the land cost me nothing, so if it should prove to be worthless I shall have suffered no loss."

"I think the property would merit investigating," Mrs. Donnelly declared firmly. "In fact, it may prove to be more valuable than anyone expects."

"Meaning what?" the lumberman demanded.

"Meaning that this land is located in a section where gold has been discovered! Few persons know of it yet, for the secret has been carefully guarded. I shouldn't disclose it, only Miss Drew befriended me today, and I always like to repay favors."

Marcus Taylor whistled softly.

"Nancy Drew, it looks to me as if you really won a prize when you selected that lucky radio title. If it should turn out that there's gold on your land, you may make a fortune!"

A faraway look had come over Nancy's face. Her eyes grew brilliant.

"Gold," she said half to herself. "That settles it! Now I know I'm going to Wellington Lake, and we can't start too soon to suit me!"

CHAPTER III

A DESIRABLE PAPER

IN GLANCING through the mail the following morning, Nancy was pleasantly surprised to find a brief note from Mrs. Taylor, requesting Carson Drew and herself to take dinner with her and Mr. Taylor at their home that evening.

"How nice of her to ask us!" she exclaimed in delight. "You'll be able to go, won't you, Father?"

"I think I can make it," the lawyer promised. "It will give me an opportunity to talk with Mrs. Donnelly, and discover if she will make a satisfactory chaperon for your Northern trip."

"She'll prove satisfactory as far as I'm concerned. I know that. If what she says is true about the finding of gold——"

"I'd not put much stock in that story, Nancy. It's not likely that a company would give away such a valuable piece of land."

"Not if they suspected it to be extremely valuable, of course. I suppose it is foolish of me to hope, yet I can't help but feel lucky about this property. What's more, if Bess and

George go with me, I know I'll have an exciting trip.''

Nancy had told her chums about the proposed vacation the previous day. Both girls were very eager to go, and now when Nancy called at the Marvin home shortly after breakfast, she found them there discussing the prospects.

''All aboard for Lake Wellington!'' George greeted her gaily.

''Will you really be able to go?'' Nancy questioned eagerly.

''I think so. Mother has practically consented.''

''How about you, Bess?''

''I don't know yet. I've been coaxing and coaxing, but my parents are very conservative. They're afraid it's too long a trip for three girls to make by themselves.''

''We won't be alone,'' Nancy said. ''Mrs. Donnelly has promised to take us if our parents wish.''

''If I don't go, I'll be just sick about it,'' Bess declared disconsolately.

''Cheer up,'' Nancy encouraged. ''I'll have Father talk with your parents. That may help.''

The girls fell to discussing various details of the proposed trip, including the clothes they were to take along. Bess was inclined to want to pack her best dresses, but Nancy discouraged her, pointing out that they would need sturdy shoes and rough, warm garments in the woods. Presently she glanced at the clock, and was startled to see how quickly time had passed.

"I must hurry home," she announced, rising. "I promised Hannah I'd bake a chocolate cake for luncheon. If I don't get started with it soon I'll never get it ready in time."

She found kindly Mrs. Gruen, the middle-aged housekeeper, busy in the spic-and-span white kitchen.

"I thought you wouldn't be here, Nancy," she remarked, as the girl donned an apron. "I'd have stirred up the cake myself, only the ones I make never come out as well as yours do."

"Flatterer!" Nancy laughed. "It was you who taught me how to bake chocolate cake."

"So I did, but the pupil has gone beyond the master. Oh, by the way, there was a telephone call for you this morning."

"From one of the girls?"

"No, it was from a man. He wouldn't give me his name."

"That's strange. Doubtless it was a salesman."

Nancy forgot about the phone call as she busied herself with the cake. She was to recall the incident later, however, and to speculate upon its significance.

Promptly at seven that evening the Drews presented themselves at the Taylor home, where they were warmly welcomed. Nancy was delighted to observe that her father and Mrs. Donnelly took an instant liking to each other. During dinner the conversation centered about his daughter's newly-acquired property.

"I shouldn't mind owning that property myself," Mrs. Donnelly smiled warmly at Nancy. "It may turn out to be worthless, yet it presents a wonderful speculation, in my opinion. If there should be gold——"

She did not finish the sentence, for a servant at that moment entered the room to say that Nancy was wanted on the telephone. Excusing herself, the girl went to answer the call, and she was away several minutes. When she returned everyone noticed the strange expression on her face.

"Father, did you ever hear of a man named Raymond Niles?" she asked quickly, as she resumed her place at the table.

The lawyer shook his head.

"It's strange," Nancy went on. "He wanted to buy my property."

"How much did he offer you for it?" Mr. Drew questioned.

"A hundred dollars."

"He must be a swindler!" Mrs. Donnelly announced, before the lawyer could offer a similar opinion. "If the land is worth a cent it's worth far more than that."

"That's what I thought," Nancy said quietly. "I told him my ground wasn't for sale."

"Did that satisfy him?" her father asked.

"No. Then he also asked to see my deed. He was very persistent."

"I'd have nothing whatever to do with him, Nancy."

"I don't intend to. I made him understand that I would not show the paper to anyone. I probably won't hear from him again."

In this hopeful opinion Nancy was destined to be greatly mistaken. The following afternoon as she was walking slowly toward the public library, a handsome young man with curly blond hair and a sophisticated smile accosted her at a street corner.

"Miss Drew, I believe?"

"Yes," Nancy assented, trying not to stare at the youth's clothes, which were in the height of fashion, and cut far too elegant an appearance for River Heights.

"I am Raymond Niles," he declared disarmingly.

Nancy stiffened.

"I am sorry, Mr. Niles, but I do not care to sell my property to you."

"Oh, I understand that, Miss Drew. But it adjoins some land which a friend of mine owns in Canada, and for a certain legal reason I should like to examine the deed."

"I cannot show it to you," Nancy returned, growing annoyed. "Please permit me to pass."

Instead of standing aside, the man fell in step with her.

"I shouldn't mind paying you a small consideration——"

"As far as I am concerned, the subject is no longer of interest to me, Mr. Niles! If you don't stop annoying me I shall call a policeman!"

"All right, if that's the way you feel about it." The young man abruptly turned away. "But I'm warning you you'll be sorry later that you didn't deal with me!"

Nancy was somewhat disturbed by the incident, and reported the encounter to her father.

"I could notify the police," he told her thoughtfully, "but that would advertise the fact that your land may be valuable. It seems to me we ought to let the matter rest for a while. In any event, you will be rid of this fellow in a few days, for soon you'll be on your way to Canada."

Mr. Drew had been favorably impressed with Mrs. Donnelly, and had completed all arrangements for the Canadian woman to chaperon Nancy, Bess, and George to Wellington Lake.

After a long talk with the attorney, Mrs. Marvin had agreed that her daughter might make the trip. The girls were so excited they could hardly wait until the day scheduled for their departure should arrive.

Hannah Gruen, however, did not entirely approve of the proposed vacation.

"In my day girls stayed at home. It wasn't considered proper for them to be running all over the country alone, much less to foreign places!"

"We're not going alone," Nancy laughed, "and one cannot really speak of Canada as a foreign country."

"Just the same, I don't know what your father is thinking of to let you go! It isn't safe up there in the woods. You may get lost, or something else terrible may happen. Mark my words!"

"Mrs. Donnelly has lived at Wellington Lake most of her life, and she's older than you!" Nancy chuckled. "I'll send you a postcard every week so you'll know I'm still alive and healthy."

Two days before the scheduled departure, Raymond Niles telephoned the Drew home.

"You haven't changed your mind about that deed?" he inquired a trifle insolently.

"No, Mr. Niles!" Nancy retorted. She hung up the receiver before he could continue the conversation.

The precious document reposed in the top drawer of a desk in Mr. Drew's study. Nancy would have felt better about it if it had been placed in a less obvious hideaway. However, it seemed foolish to go to the trouble of taking it to the bank vault for such a brief period, since she intended to carry it with her on her journey North.

Time was growing short, and Nancy was too busy packing to give much thought to Raymond Niles. Once Bess had caught the fellow lurking about the Drew home. A dozen times a day the cousins would run over to the house to chat excitedly about the trip, or to seek advice concerning their wardrobes.

"Everything is ready," Nancy informed Hannah as she finished strapping the last bag. "Our train leaves at seven tonight, and I'm going to the bank now for some money. If anyone should call while I'm away, tell him I'll be back in half an hour."

She was gone from the house longer than she had anticipated. Upon returning a little past four o'clock, she entered the kitchen to find it deserted.

"Hannah!" she called.

"Coming," the housekeeper rejoined from the general direction of the study. An instant later the woman bustled into the room.

"Oh, Nancy, I'm so glad you've returned," she began anxiously, "for I didn't know what to do when that man came for the paper you promised him."

"What paper?" the girl asked quickly.

"A deed you keep in the desk drawer. This chap was mighty handsome, and said he was a good friend of yours."

"You didn't give the paper to him?" Nancy demanded in alarm.

"Yes, I did, but he's still in the library, for I told him to wait there. Oh, I hope I haven't done anything wrong!"

Nancy darted toward the study. As she had feared, it was empty. Raymond Niles had tricked Hannah!

Panic-stricken at the thought of losing the valuable paper, Nancy raced toward the front door. She caught a glimpse of the man moving hurriedly across the porch.

"Wait!" she called sharply.

As he wheeled about, the girl sprang forward and caught him by the arm.

"Give me my deed!" she cried.

The man tried to thrust the document into his pocket, but Nancy snatched it from him.

"You are a trickster!" she accused the fellow. "Leave this house at once, or I'll turn you over to the police!"

Raymond Niles muttered something Nancy could not catch. She closed the door in his face.

"I thought he was a friend of yours, or I'd

never have trusted him," Hannah said in distress. "I couldn't have forgiven myself if I'd have let him steal that deed."

"Don't worry about it now," the girl returned kindly. "It wasn't your fault. Anyway, I saved it, and that's all that matters."

The few remaining hours before train time passed all too swiftly. Many friends telephoned Nancy to bid her good-bye, while an even greater number gathered at the railroad station to speed the girls on their journey. Hannah was quite tearful as she bade her young mistress farewell.

"I won't rest a minute until you're safe back in River Heights," she declared.

Nancy glanced uneasily about the station platform. It seemed to her that everyone in River Heights had gathered there—that is to say, all save her father. She wondered what could be keeping him. He had telephoned her at the house, telling her he would meet her at the station; but the block signal now warned her the train was approaching, and still Mr. Drew had not appeared.

"What can be delaying Father?" she fretted. "I can't start off without saying good-bye to him."

At that instant Bess caught sight of the attorney driving up in a taxi. Nancy rushed over to greet him.

"What kept you?" she asked tremulously.

"I was afraid you weren't going to get here in time."

"So was I," Carson Drew returned, clasping her hand. "Nancy, several things have happened since I saw you last. I'm not sure but that it's a mistake to allow you to make this trip——"

"Oh, Father——"

"I'll not change my mind about it now, but I must warn you to be very careful. I'm a trifle uneasy over this land of yours."

"I don't understand."

"There's something going on that I don't exactly like." Carson Drew spoke hurriedly, for the train was almost in. "I just learned that Tom Stripe is out of jail on bond."

"But what has that to do with my land?"

"Perhaps nothing. However, bond was furnished by Raymond Niles."

"Indicating that they are friends and crooks."

"Undoubtedly. Now, the association may mean nothing at all, but while you're at Wellington Lake be on the lookout constantly for trickery."

"I shall do so," Nancy promised seriously.

Carson Drew bent down to kiss his daughter good-bye as the train came thundering into the station. A moment later Nancy stepped aboard, and with Mrs. Donnelly and her chums she began the long journey to Wellington Lake.

CHAPTER IV

A TRAIN WRECK

MRS. DONNELLY ordered her berth made up shortly after she boarded the train. Nancy and her chums were far too excited to sleep, however. They wandered into the observation car, where they interested themselves with various magazines and newspapers.

Soon Nancy became absorbed in a fascinating story entitled "The Vital Hour," but casually glanced up from her reading as a distinguished-looking woman of about thirty-five entered the car, and took a seat near by.

"I see you are reading one of my stories," the newcomer presently remarked.

Nancy looked up with interest.

"Then your name is——"

"That particular story is published under a nom de plume. As a rule I use my own name, Ann Chapelle."

Nancy stared.

"You're not Ann Chapelle who wrote the story for the Velvet Hour?"

"Yes, I am," the other smiled.

"Why, I follow them all over the radio! If

it hadn't been for you, I shouldn't be on this train now. You see, I won the mystery story title contest and am on my way to Wellington Lake, Canada, to look over the piece of property which I was awarded.''

It was Miss Chapelle's turn to be astonished.

''Then you must be Nancy Drew! I knew your title had been selected, but I never dreamed I'd ever meet you in person.''

''Do you expect to write another radio skit soon?'' Nancy inquired hopefully.

''Not for some time, I imagine. I am now busy with a novel, and my movie contracts keep me occupied steadily.''

''Then you write scenarios, too?''

''Yes, that is the type of work I like best.''

''You must know many of the famous actors and actresses.''

''I do,'' Miss Chapelle acknowledged. ''However, I must confess I attend but few parties. I don't care a great deal for social activities.''

The woman lapsed into a moody silence which Nancy hesitated to interrupt. She suspected that Miss Chapelle had some secret sorrow about which the public knew nothing. Despite her interesting life, the young writer seemed to be very unhappy.

''I hope you will find time to read my latest novel when it is published,'' Miss Chapelle remarked a few minutes later. ''But then, I may

decide not to bring it out after all, for it is too
revealing. It follows very minutely the unhappy pattern of my own life.''

Nancy was on the point of asking a question,
but the words died upon her lips, for suddenly
there came a shrill whistle from the train engine, followed by a terrific crash. Nancy was
flung headlong from her seat. Splintered
boards, battered furniture and debris descended upon her.

For a moment the girl was too stunned to
move. Then, as she squirmed to a sitting position she became aware of a sharp pain in her
arm. Carefully she moved it, relieved to discover that it had not been broken. A trickle
of blood oozed from a cut in her forehead.

All about her she could hear people groaning. The first panic-stricken screams of the
passengers had died away; cries of suffering
had taken their place.

The Drew girl staggered to her feet, looking about her for Bess and George. The latter
was half hidden under a pile of observation car
chairs.

''I'll get you out in a minute,'' Nancy encouraged.

A moment later she helped the stunned girl
to her feet.

''What happened?'' George murmured in bewilderment.

''There's been a wreck. Are you hurt?''

"Only shaken up a bit, I think. Is Bess safe?"

"I haven't found her yet."

"She was sitting right beside me when the crash came."

Anxiously the girls began to move the debris, peering carefully beneath each pile. A low moan drew them to the place where their chum lay. Her face was so white they thought she must be seriously injured.

"Bess!" Nancy dropped to her knees.

"Where am I?" the victim mumbled incoherently.

Tenderly the girls lifted her and carried her to a level spot outside the car. Nancy chaffed her friend's hands and spread out her coat for Bess to lie upon.

"Don't bother about me," she directed presently. "I'm dazed from a blow I received on the head, but I'll soon be all right. Help the others."

"Let's try to find Mrs. Donnelly and Miss Chapelle," Nancy suggested.

Anxiously she and George looked about for the two women, but did not see them among the little group of those uninjured. Returning to the observation car, they aided a child who had been pinned under a steel beam, and lifted out a boy with a broken leg.

Almost every car had jumped the track. Nancy noted that the coach which Mrs. Don-

nelly had occupied had received the brunt of
the impact. Nearby sections were afire. The
flames, whipped by a strong south wind, were
spreading rapidly.

"Get some helpers and see if you can find
Miss Chapelle," Nancy called to George. "I'll
make certain that Mrs. Donnelly is safe."

It was difficult for Nancy to ignore the pitiful
cries of the injured passengers as she hurried
past them, yet she felt that her first duty was
to her friends. If Mrs. Donnelly had been
trapped in her berth, she might be burned to
death.

The car she was in had been converted into a
tangled, twisted mass of steel. Nancy grew
bewildered as she tried to locate the place
where her chaperon might be. Flames were
creeping ever closer and closer.

"Won't you help me?" she appealed to a
man near by. "I am afraid a woman is
trapped inside this car."

The fellow shook his head regretfully.

"I must search for my own little daughter
first. The wrecking crew will be along soon."

"It may be too late then," Nancy thought
desperately.

Over and over she called Mrs. Donnelly's
name, but there was no response. All about
her women were crying hysterically, while chil-
dren were sobbing and searching for their parents. Nancy felt physically ill, yet she

continued pulling away debris, working desperately to beat the creeping line of red flame.

Just then George came running back to help her.

"Have you found Miss Chapelle?" Nancy asked.

"No. I've hunted everywhere. I'd have kept on looking, only I thought you might need me here."

"I do. Oh, George, I'm afraid we'll not get to her in time——"

At that moment a glad shout went up, for the wrecking crew had been sighted!

"Thank goodness, they've come at last!" Nancy exclaimed.

Even as she spoke, a burning brand, carried by the wind, dropped at her feet. She stamped it out, but still others fell about her.

In another minute the car would be afire!

CHAPTER V

DISASTER

NANCY and George stood helplessly by, watching the wrecking crew at work. The girls had done all they possibly could to assist the injured passengers; now they must wait and hope.

In response to Nancy's frantic plea the wrecking crew had bravely battled the fire, removing several persons from the flaming car Mrs. Donnelly had occupied. The chaperon, however, had not been among those rescued.

"Are you sure she was in this coach?" one of the workers asked Nancy.

"Yes. She occupied section fourteen. I know she was inside at the time of the crash."

"We may find her yet," the man returned with forced cheerfulness, "but it does look bad."

"It's possible she was rescued before we got here," George said hopefully.

Nancy nodded, trying all the while to keep up her spirits. She could not acknowledge to herself that Mrs. Donnelly might be dead.

The night was very black, the only illumina-

tion being that provided by torches and lan-
terns brought along by the wrecking crew.
Many of the injured passengers had been removed to hospitals and nearby houses. It was
possible that in the confusion they had failed
to see Mrs. Donnelly. This hope gave them
fresh courage.

"We may as well go back to Bess," Nancy
proposed, "for we can do no good here."

The girls found Bess in much better condition than when they had left her. She was
wrapped in a warm blanket to protect her from
the cold night air.

"How is Mrs. Donnelly?" she asked instantly.

It was not easy to tell her the truth.

"She hasn't been found yet," Nancy said
quietly. "But we still have hope."

Bess was silent for a time; then she said
soberly:

"This wreck has been a terrible thing. It
was dreadful to sit here and see the workers
carrying people past on stretchers. I hate to
think that anything has happened to Mrs. Donnelly or to that new acquaintance of yours,
Nancy."

"Miss Chapelle?"

"Yes. She hasn't been found, either."

"I don't believe she was seriously injured,
for almost everyone in the observation car es-

caped lightly," Nancy said thoughtfully. "It's a mystery what became of her."

"A great many strange things have happened tonight," Bess declared significantly. "For instance, what could have caused the wreck?"

"The men said it was an open switch," George told her.

"I suppose it was an accident, all right," Bess agreed, "but I grew suspicious when I saw Raymond Niles and another fellow in the throng here tonight!"

Nancy and George exchanged quick glances. They could not decide if Bess actually had seen Niles and a companion, or if she had imagined it. Bess guessed what the two girls were thinking.

"Oh, I know you believe I was too dazed to recognize anyone! But I did see Raymond Niles."

"Can you describe his companion?" Nancy questioned.

"Not very well, I'm afraid. He was about forty years of age, I should say. A dapper sort of man, though not as well dressed as Niles."

Nancy recalled the information her father had given her just as the train had pulled into the River Heights station. Raymond Niles had provided bail for Tom Stripe. Bess's description fitted the latter very well. Could it be possible that the two had boarded the train with the intention of following Nancy to Wellington Lake?

"I must be on my guard," she thought, "but I'll not worry Bess and George by telling them what I fear. If anything has happened to Mrs. Donnelly, we'll not go to Canada now, anyway."

For nearly an hour the three girls remained at the scene of the wreck. At the end of that period Nancy's nerves began to give way under the strain. It was then that her friends observed that she, too, had been injured.

"You must see a doctor immediately," Bess insisted.

"It's nothing," Nancy maintained. "I'll be quite all right after a night's rest. If we only knew what has become of Mrs. Donnelly and Miss Chapelle!"

"You'll make yourself ill if you don't stop worrying," George advised her kindly. "I can't help but feel they are both safe."

"We should know the worst by morning," Nancy said quietly. "There is no purpose in our remaining here. I suggest that we spend the remainder of the night at a hotel. I am sure there must be one in the vicinity."

The others readily agreed to the suggestion, for they were exhausted from their harrowing experiences. A conveyance carried them to a nearby town, where they engaged a room at the Hamilton Hotel.

Before retiring, Nancy sent a telegram to her father, telling him that she was safe. Bess and George dispatched similar messages to their parents.

"I believe I'll not be able to sleep a wink," Bess declared nervously, as her chums tucked blankets about her. "I feel positively unnerved."

"So do I," Nancy acknowledged, "but we should be thankful we're alive and uninjured."

"And that our luggage wasn't destroyed," George added. "Nancy, did you manage to save your property papers?"

"Yes, they were in my purse, which I never let out of my hand."

Nancy indicated the pocketbook which lay on the dresser. Bess regarded it fixedly, then closed her eyes and dropped off into a troubled sleep.

George, too, was so exhausted that she fell into a deep slumber almost the instant her head touched the pillow. At first Nancy was so restless and worried that she could not sleep, though presently she dozed off.

She awoke when it was yet dark, to experience a strange sensation. It seemed as though someone had called to her.

Sitting up, she looked about the hotel room. George was sleeping peacefully at her side.

She looked toward the bed occupied by Bess, but it was empty.

Thoroughly alarmed, Nancy thrust aside the covers and sprang to the floor. She tried the outside door and found it still locked from the inside. She next ran to the open window. A low cry of horror escaped her as she gazed downward.

Bess, apparently walking in her sleep, had climbed out upon the fire escape. Then she had descended until she was on a level with a window ledge. At the moment she stood teetering upon the narrow slab of concrete! At any instant she might plunge to her death!

Nancy's low cry had disturbed George. "What is it?" she murmured drowsily.

"Don't make a sound," Nancy warned fearfully. "Come here."

George crept to the open window. As she beheld the sight below, she stifled an exclamation of fear.

"If we awaken her she will be sure to fall," Nancy whispered, shuddering as she glanced down at the garden several feet below. "I'm going to try to get to her."

It was a mystery how Bess had managed to climb over to the narrow ledge. She was poised far out of reach. Even from the fire escape Nancy could not assume the same position without risking her own life.

"I'll have to try some other way," she decided, returning to the bedroom window.

"We can never rescue her alone," George said. "I'll run downstairs for help."

She drew on a robe, then disappeared.

Left to herself, Nancy watched Bess fearfully. The girl would be safe if she would remain where she was, but at any moment she might take a step forward, which would send her hurtling into the garden.

Unable to endure the suspense of waiting for help, Nancy rushed to an upstairs hall. Her eyes suddenly fell upon a coiled rope that a workman had left that day. Snatching it up, she ran to a window directly over the spot where Bess was standing.

A minute later George, followed by two frightened hotel attendants, raced back into the vacant bedroom.

"There she is!" George cried, as she pointed out the ghostly white figure upon the ledge.

Her words ended in a shrill scream. Bess's foot had slipped. The horrified observers saw her pitch forward and fall toward the garden!

CHAPTER VI

The Lost Note

A rope swished through the air, and settled neatly about Bess's shoulders. From the hall window above Nancy drew it tight, and held the girl back against the ledge.

The near fall had awakened Bess. Becoming aware of her situation, she uttered a terrified cry for help, and cringed against the wall.

"Don't move! We'll get you in a minute," Nancy warned.

George and the two men had already lowered themselves upon the fire escape. With Nancy aiding from above by the skillful use of her rope, they managed to reach the frightened girl, and escort her back to the bedroom. Bess slumped down in a little heap.

"I was never so frightened before in all my life! Nancy, if you hadn't thrown that rope when you did, I'd surely have been killed."

"That was just a little trick I learned a couple of years ago at Shadow Ranch. Fortunately, I didn't miss my aim."

After the two attendants had left, the girls plied Bess with questions.

"I have no more idea than you have why I did it," Bess told them ruefully. "As far as I know, I have never before walked in my sleep. I suppose it was because I was so upset about the wreck. And I had such an awful nightmare."

"What was it like?" George asked curiously.

"Oh, I can't remember the first part of it—but some dreadful animal seemed to be pursuing me. Then the dream shifted, and I thought someone was after Nancy's papers."

"That was because I mentioned them just before you went to sleep," Nancy smiled.

"I suppose so. Anyway, I thought I'd get up and put them in a safer place. I remember going over to the dresser. The next moment I woke up to find myself on that ledge." Bess shuddered again at the realization of what might have happened to her.

Being reminded of the precious deed to her property, Nancy glanced toward the dresser expecting to find her purse where she had left it, but it was not there.

"Bess, you don't suppose you actually picked up the pocketbook, do you?" she inquired anxiously, looking about the room.

Almost at once she saw the purse lying open on the carpet, and snatched it up. One glance inside revealed that the deed was missing.

"Oh, what have I done!" Bess exclaimed in distress. "You don't suppose I actually took your papers and hid them somewhere, do you?"

"It begins to look as if you did," Nancy was forced to say ruefully.

George was struck by a sudden thought.

"I seem to recall that Bess held something white in her hand when we first saw her standing on that ledge! Perhaps she dropped the deed into the garden."

"Yes, and I noticed something flutter to the ground just as I threw the rope," Nancy added with reviving hope.

"I'll find out if it's lying in the garden now," George declared.

She crossed over to the window and peered down. Involuntarily she emitted a low exclamation of dismay.

"What is it?" Nancy cried, springing to her friend's side.

She caught a glimpse of a man retreating down the alley.

"I saw him pick up a paper from beneath the window!" George announced tensely. "I was too startled to call out until he had moved away. Oh, Nancy, I'm just as sure as anything that it was your lost deed!"

"It's useless to go after him, for he's too far away now," Nancy said in a discouraged tone. "I suppose the paper is lost and with it my chances of ever claiming my Canadian property."

"It's all my fault," Bess accused herself

gloomily. "If I had the money, I'd pay you for that land."

Nancy squeezed her chum's hand.

"Don't feel bad about it, Bess. After all that's happened tonight, the property doesn't seem as important to me as it did before."

"But to think that I deliberately threw away your papers! I don't understand how I could have done such a crazy thing, even in my sleep."

"There's a possibility the deed will be returned," Nancy remarked thoughtfully. "At any rate, I'll run an ad in the paper tomorrow. The man who picked up the document may see it and apply for a reward."

Bess felt too upset over the entire matter to go back to sleep. Since it was almost five o'clock, the girls finished their dressing and sent downstairs for hot coffee. As soon as the dining room opened they had breakfast. Yet, despite Nancy's attempts to keep up a cheerful conversation, a feeling of deep gloom prevailed.

At their first opportunity the girls dispatched an advertisement to the local paper, offering a reward for the return of the missing deed. Scarcely had they finished telephoning, than the hotel clerk called them over to the desk.

"I have good news for you at last," he told the girls cheerfully.

"Our friends have been saved?" Bess gasped.

"Yes. Mrs. Donnelly and Miss Chapelle are both at the Good Hope Hospital."

"They're not seriously injured?" Nancy questioned anxiously.

"I couldn't learn that. The best thing for you to do will be to hire a car and drive out there. It isn't more than five miles into the country."

"We'll start just as soon as we can find a means of conveyance," Nancy decided.

With the aid of the helpful clerk they found a driver, who for a nominal sum agreed to take them to the Good Hope Hospital. As they were leaving town Nancy caught a glimpse of the newspaper office.

"Stop here just a minute," she directed the driver, and explained to Bess and George, "I want to run in and see if my advertisement has been copied correctly."

She vanished into the building, to return within a few minutes, a letter clutched in her hand. Triumphantly she flashed it before George and Bess.

"It couldn't be an answer to your advertisement!" the latter gasped. "That would be impossible, because the paper hasn't been issued yet!"

"Shortly after I telephoned this morning, a man came into the office and left this letter.

He told the editor to give it to anyone claiming to have lost an important paper near the Hamilton Hotel!"

"What does the note say?" George demanded impatiently.

Nancy ripped open the cheap envelope and scanned the brief message. She looked slightly disappointed.

"Why, it doesn't say a thing about the lost deed. It just asks me to call at the Ranny farm six miles south of Windham."

"Where is Windham?" Bess questioned curiously of the taxi man.

"This is Windham," the driver informed her, a tinge of scorn in his voice.

"We didn't think of inquiring the name of the town last night," Bess said apologetically. "We were so upset on account of the wreck."

"Windham is one of the nicest little places in the U. S. A.," the driver went on proudly. "Not far from the Canadian border, either."

"We must drive out to the Ranny farm at the first opportunity," Nancy decided. "If it should happen that my deed has been recovered, I'll feel greatly relieved."

"If you get the paper back, we may be able to go on to Wellington Lake a little later," George added a trifle wistfully. "Just think— if everything hadn't gone wrong we'd be there now."

A brief ride over bumpy dirt roads brought

the girls to the Good Hope Hospital, a county institution. Entering the lobby, they anxiously inquired for their friends.

"Mrs. Donnelly is doing very well," they were informed by the girl at the desk. "Unfortunately, we can't say as much for Miss Chapelle. She has been seriously injured, and is suffering from the loss of a great deal of blood."

The girls were led into Mrs. Donnelly's room. The patient was overjoyed at seeing them.

"I couldn't sleep last night for worrying about you," the woman declared. "Had one of you been injured, I never could have faced your parents."

"And we spent the night worrying about you," Nancy smiled.

"I don't wonder you did, for I was whisked away to this hospital almost before I knew I had been hurt. I had just gone to the dressing room when the crash came. I was thrown to the floor and must have lost consciousness. In any event, when I came to I was in a car being transported to this place. I learned later that I was the first person taken from the wreck."

"Are you feeling better?" Nancy inquired.

"Yes indeed. The doctor tells me I'll be able to leave here in a few days."

The girls talked with Mrs. Donnelly a while longer. Presently a nurse came to warn them that they must not tire the patient by remaining over their allotted fifteen minutes.

"May we see Miss Chapelle?" Nancy asked, when they were again in the corridor.

The nurse hesitated.

"If you wish to do so, you may go in for a minute or two, but that is all. Be careful not to excite her, for her condition is grave."

Nancy was shocked as she entered Miss Chapelle's room. The authoress, swathed in bandages, scarcely moved a muscle as the girls approached her bed. Yet as Nancy bent over the pale, wan face, a gleam of recognition flashed into the woman's pain-stricken eyes.

"I'm near the end," she murmured, very low.

"You mustn't say that," Nancy told her encouragingly. "Of course you'll get well again."

Miss Chapelle shook her head.

"I shall die—I know it. I am glad you came, for there is something I must tell you."

Her voice dropped to a whisper. Nancy moved nearer, that she might not miss a word.

"It's the story of—" The woman faltered; she could not finish. She closed her eyes, completely exhausted.

"Don't try to tell me now," Nancy said compassionately.

Even as she spoke, she realized that there might never be another time in which to hear the story. The authoress was sinking rapidly.

Miss Chapelle made one last desperate attempt to speak, raising up her head.

"The message—in the hollow oak—" she muttered.

Then she dropped back upon the pillow, and lapsed into unconsciousness.

CHAPTER VII

A CLUE TO THE DEED

NANCY and her chums huddled in the barren corridor outside of Miss Chapelle's room. Doctors and attendants went in and out, their faces tense, but no one took time to pause and tell the girls if the authoress was still alive.

"As long as the doctors keep working over her, she must be living," Bess declared with forced cheerfulness.

"What was it she whispered?" George asked. "I was too far from the bed to catch the words."

"She said, 'The message in the Hollow Oak,'" Nancy informed her. "What that means I don't know."

"She must have been delirious," Bess said.

Nancy was on the point of disagreeing, when the door opened and the nurse quietly stepped into the corridor. She walked rapidly toward the girls.

"How is she?" Nancy asked fearfully.

"We thought the end had come, but by some miracle she has rallied."

"Then there is hope?" Nancy inquired.

"Yes, Miss Chapelle is sleeping quietly now, but of course the danger is not past. If you are acquainted with her friends or relatives, I suggest you wire them immediately."

Nancy was forced to acknowledge that she could not provide the hospital with the names. However, she was struck with a sudden thought.

"Miss Chapelle came from Hollywood. It's possible that someone in the moving picture colony knows of her family. Or, you might get in touch with one of the magazines for which she writes."

"Thank you for your suggestion," the nurse said gratefully. "We'll try both leads."

Since they could be of no assistance by remaining at the hospital, the girls returned to the Hamilton Hotel.

"What are our plans to be?" George asked gloomily, as they discussed matters in their room. "Shall we return to River Heights?"

"We shouldn't go away and leave Mrs. Donnelly," Nancy said. "Anyway, from what the nurse told me I rather think she'll be able to travel again in a few days."

"Then do you think we might go on into Canada?" Bess questioned eagerly.

"If Mrs. Donnelly fully recovers I think we can; that is, if I get my deed back. Of course, without the paper it would be foolish of me to go on to Wellington Lake."

"Why not drive out to the Ranny farm this afternoon?" George proposed.

"I had thought of it. We're not doing Mrs. Donnelly or Miss Chapelle any good by remaining at the hospital, and the excursion will help fill in our time."

The girls were a trifle worried concerning their finances. Although their parents had given them ample funds for the journey to Lake Wellington, they had not figured on additional hotel bills and frequent taxi fares to and from the county hospital. Nancy suggested that they might save money by engaging a car and driving it themselves. However, they were less enthusiastic about the idea when they saw the old automobile that was assigned to them.

"Do you think it will hold together long enough for us to get to the Ranny farm?" Bess asked doubtfully.

"That car's been running for nearly ten years now," the owner informed her, irritated by her manner. "You're the first folks that ever complained about it."

"Oh, we're not complaining," Nancy said hastily. "If you'll show me how to start the engine, I think we can manage very well."

Bess and George refused to have anything to do with the intricate mechanism of the old vehicle, so Nancy was obliged to take the wheel. Before leaving town she inquired the way to the Ranny farm.

"Take the first turn south," she was told glibly, "then turn north at Fisher's farm, cross the Little Bear Creek, go south again for quite a piece, and angle off a bit to the west until you come to a crooked lane. Follow it for maybe a mile, and you'll be there!"

"Just as clear as mud," Nancy laughingly reported to her chums. "I suspect this trip will turn out to be a pioneering expedition after all."

Before they had gone two miles a rear tire blew out. It took the girls almost three-quarters of an hour to fix it, for some of the necessary tools were missing. When the tire had been changed, they had difficulty in starting the car again, for Nancy was not used to the temperamental tricks of the engine.

At length the motor began to roar and the girls continued down the dusty road. They had no way of knowing how far they had traveled, for the speedometer was broken.

"It seems to me we've gone at least ten miles," George maintained. "I know we've taken a wrong turn somewhere."

"I suppose we have," Nancy sighed, stopping the car. "I think I'll walk over to that farmhouse on the hill and get directions."

Unwilling to be left behind, Bess and George insisted upon walking with their chum, who proposed that they cut through a pasture to save time. They crawled under a fence and struck out across the fields. Only after they had gone quite a distance did they notice a bull quietly grazing in the far end of the field.

"O-oh," Bess squealed in fright, "let's turn back!"

"It will be farther to the road than to the house," Nancy pointed out.

"That old bull won't hurt you," George teased. "He isn't even looking this way."

But as she spoke the animal raised its head. Terrified, Bess started to run. Her red sweater infuriated the animal. With a snort of rage, it came toward the girls.

"Run for your lives!" Nancy shouted.

The three girls raced madly for the fence. Heavy hoofs pounded behind them. As she glanced over her shoulder, Nancy saw that soon the bull would be upon them. They might reach the fence, but they would never have sufficient time to climb over it.

"Hurry, and you'll make it!" a masculine voice shouted.

The girls noticed a big wooden gate, and could see a farmer who was swinging it open for them. They darted through, fairly collapsing at his feet. Then the gate slammed after them, and they were safe.

"What do you mean by frightening my bull?" the man demanded crossly.

The girls stared at him, then burst into laughter.

"We thought it was the other way around," Nancy managed to say, as she tried to regain her breath.

"Didn't you see that sign on the fence that said to keep out?"

"We didn't see any sign," Nancy maintained. "We were driving along the road and noticed your house. We wanted to ask the way to the Ranny farm, and thought we'd take a short cut through the field."

It was the farmer's turn to stare.

"You're at the Ranny farm now," he said.

"And are you Mr. Ranny?" Nancy questioned. "The man who left the letter at the newspaper office?"

"Yes, I am. Who be you?"

Nancy told him her name and introduced her chums. The farmer softened considerably after they explained their mission.

"Yes, I have the paper safe in the house," he admitted. "I was taking the milk and some produce to town early in the morning, when I saw the document lyin' on the grass. Soon as I looked at it I knew it was something important, so I wrote that letter and left it at the newspaper office. Figured someone would be advertising before long."

"I'd like to give you a reward," Nancy promised.

The farmer looked as if he had been insulted.

"I don't want any reward. You're welcome to the paper if it belongs to you."

"Oh, thank you," Nancy said gratefully. "I can prove that it is mine, for it is a deed to my property in Canada."

"Come along, then, and I'll give it to you."

He led the girls into a comfortable cottage and introduced them to a stout, pleasant-faced woman who was baking pie in the kitchen. She greeted the girls cordially, chatting amiably with them while her husband found the deed he had put away in the desk.

"A dreadful wreck, wasn't it?" Mrs. Ranny began conversationally.

"Indeed it was," Nancy agreed. "We were in it, too."

She then told of their experiences. The farmer's wife listened spellbound.

"I feel so sorry for the poor passengers who were hurt," Mrs. Ranny said sympathetically. "I said to my husband this morning, I only wished we might do something to help."

"Perhaps you can," Nancy returned, as a plan occurred to her. Before she could tell what it was, Mr. Ranny came with the deed.

"Here you are, Miss Drew. I'm glad to be able to accommodate you."

"I wish you would accept a reward."

The farmer shook his head stubbornly, so Nancy did not urge him further.

"Won't you all stay to dinner?" Mrs. Ranny asked cordially. "We're having steak that we butchered ourselves."

The delightful aroma of food cooking was too much for Nancy and her chums to resist. After a little urging they gratefully accepted the invitation to remain.

The girls were not mistaken in thinking that Mrs. Ranny was an excellent cook. The food she served was plain and substantial, but well seasoned. Her guests paid her many fine compliments on it.

Nancy was eager to show her gratitude for the return of the lost deed. As she prepared to leave, she mentioned the plan which had occurred to her.

"You spoke of wanting to do something to aid the unfortunate passengers who were injured in the wreck, Mrs. Ranny. As it happens, we have a friend who was slightly hurt. She is at the Good Hope Hospital now but expects to leave within a day or two. She should go to a place where she can have a complete rest. If you would care to have her here, I am sure that some arrangement might be worked out."

"I should indeed be glad to have her come here," Mrs. Ranny said without an instant's hesitation. "I don't mind saying we need money. And this is a quiet place for an invalid. We have plenty of milk and eggs."

"Then I'll talk over the idea with her and let you know," Nancy promised, turning to leave.

When Mrs. Donnelly was informed of the plan, she grew more than enthusiastic. Although Miss Chapelle's condition remained unchanged, the older woman had improved rapidly. The doctors agreed that she might leave the hospital whenever she wished.

"Then we'll take you down to the farm tomorrow," Nancy promised her. "I know you'll love the place, for it is very clean and pleasant."

At three the next afternoon a comfortable touring car brought Mrs. Donnelly and the girls to the Ranny place. Nancy was delighted to find that the invalid seemed highly pleased with the surroundings. However, when Mrs. Ranny came hurrying out of the house to greet the party, the girl was destined for a severe shock.

"Mrs. Ranny, this is Mrs. Donnelly," said Nancy pleasantly.

The only response to her introduction was a chilly silence. The two women were staring at each other, bitter hatred in their eyes.

"Take me back to the hospital!" Mrs. Donnelly ordered sharply. "Never in the world will I stay here!"

CHAPTER VIII

An Ancient Feud

Gradually Nancy sensed that by bringing Mrs. Donnelly to the home of Mrs. Ranny she unwittingly had committed a grave error. Undoubtedly an old feud existed between the two women. Where they had met, or what had caused the trouble she had no idea; yet there was no question but that at the present moment the two were bitter enemies.

Nancy would have made an effort to effect a reconciliation had it seemed at all possible to do so, but the way the two glared at each other so angrily she felt it would be useless for her to attempt it.

"Take me away from here!" Mrs. Donnelly commanded.

Nancy ordered the driver to go back to the Hamilton Hotel. For some time the little party rode on in silence, the girls waiting for Mrs. Donnelly to offer some excuse for her strange behavior. For several minutes she stared straight ahead of her and said nothing, but finally spoke up.

"I never expected to see her again in my life," she presently murmured.

The chums waited expectantly. Then she went on, a slightly bitter note in her voice:

"Her father and mine were rivals years ago at Wellington Lake. They had trouble over a tract of timber."

"And is that the reason why you harbor this ill feeling toward Mrs. Ranny?" Nancy probed gently.

"Mrs. Ranny? Is that her name now? I knew her when she was a girl—neither of us was married at the time. I guess it was natural that we should dislike each other when our fathers were at such swords' points. Probably the fight would never have been so bitter had it not been for money. But when gold is involved, people lose all sense of balance."

"Gold?" Nancy inquired alertly.

"Yes. The timber tract I mentioned is very near your land. But please don't ask me to go into detail about it now. Meeting that woman after all these years has upset me dreadfully. I don't like to talk about it."

"I'm very sorry I took you there," Nancy apologized. "I had no idea you were acquainted with Mrs. Ranny."

Mrs. Donnelly patted the girl's hand.

"There, there, don't look so distressed, child. Of course it wasn't your fault. It was just an unfortunate occurrence."

Nancy longed to ask questions about the old feud between the two families, and wanted to learn more about the competition for the timber land, but she carefully restrained herself. She could tell that Mrs. Donnelly had been greatly unnerved by the incident, and feared that the woman might break down before they could take her to the hotel.

"You must go to bed as soon as I can engage a room for you," Nancy told her. "This long ride from the hospital has been too much of a strain on you."

"I do feel exhausted. If I could just get some sleep——"

"You shall. Now, don't give Mrs. Ranny another thought," the girl added, as they reached their destination.

Nancy did not leave her until the woman had calmed down sufficiently to go to sleep. Then she returned to her chums, and the three discussed the situation together.

"I cannot figure out how we'll ever manage to go on to Wellington Lake," Bess said gloomily. "After this set-back Mrs. Donnelly may be unable to travel for a week."

"The meeting with Mrs. Ranny was unfortunate, to say the least," Nancy acknowledged. "Still, Mrs. Donnelly looked much better when I left her. I believe after another day she'll be quite like herself again."

"There's still Miss Chapelle to think of," George reminded her friend. "What are you going to do about her?"

Nancy had not forgotten her new friend. Unbeknown to Bess and George, she had left word at the hospital that should the authoress experience the slightest turn for the worse, they were to notify the Drew girl at once.

"I couldn't leave here until I was sure Miss Chapelle was out of danger," Nancy told her chums soberly. "I took such a great liking to her. Besides, she's absolutely alone."

Bess and George nodded in agreement.

"I guess we're all fretting because of the delay," Nancy went on in a more animated tone. "It seems I can't wait until we reach Canada! If there should be gold on the land——"

"That phrase has been your theme song ever since we left River Heights," George laughed.

"Gold can bring about a great many complications," Bess commented. "You have just seen how it has caused a bitter feud between Mrs. Donnelly and Mrs. Ranny."

"It seems a pity that they are estranged," Nancy murmured. "Of course, we may not know all the story, but often serious quarrels develop from mere trifles."

It was almost time for the mail to be distributed. After discussing the situation a while longer, the girls descended to the lobby. They did not really expect any letters, so were pleasantly surprised when the clerk handed each of them a fat envelope.

"Word from home!" Nancy cried joyfully, dropping down in the nearest chair to read the lengthy communication which her father had sent.

"I'm almost afraid to open mine," Bess said uneasily. "If Mother insists that I return home instead of going on to Lake Wellington, I'll be mighty disappointed."

The girls had no real reason for worrying. Although their parents had been greatly disturbed by the news of the accident, they evidently had discussed the matter together. They had concluded that since the girls were so near the Canadian border it would be much better for them to remain where they were until Mrs. Donnelly should fully recover, when they might continue according to their original plan.

"Everything is fine now," Nancy declared in relief. "Father sent me some more money. If our expenses should mount up faster than we expect, we'll still have plenty of funds."

Carson Drew had added a brief note of warning to his somewhat lengthy communication.

"Be sure," he wrote, "to keep a sharp lookout for Tom Stripe and Raymond Niles. I have reason to believe that they have left River Heights."

Nancy re-read the paragraph, recalling that Bess had maintained she had seen Niles at the time of the wreck. Had the men planned to follow her to Canada? The thought troubled her.

"Why are you scowling?" George demanded with a laugh. "Bad news from home?"

Nancy's face relaxed.

"No, I was just thinking about something— nothing important, I guess."

The girls were starting toward the elevator, when the clerk motioned for them to return to the desk.

"A telephone call for you, Miss Drew," he said.

Nancy went into a nearby booth. As she took down the receiver she found herself connected with the Good Hope Hospital.

"Miss Drew, you asked us to notify you if Miss Chapelle's condition had changed. We should like to have you come to the hospital without a moment's delay."

"Has she taken a turn for the worse?" Nancy inquired anxiously.

"Yes. The doctors have decided to operate. It's the only hope they have of saving her life."

"I'll be there in a few minutes," Nancy promised.

She returned to her chums, and quickly explained to them the situation.

"I must leave at once. I don't know when

I can get back, so perhaps you two should stay with Mrs. Donnelly in case she needs some-one."

"We'll look after her," George promised. "Oh, I do hope Miss Chapelle rallies from her operation."

Fifteen minutes later Nancy reached the county hospital, and was sent directly to the upper floor, where she was met by Miss Chapelle's day nurse.

"How is the patient?" Nancy questioned.

"As well as can be expected under the circumstances. She is rational now, and wants to talk to you before she undergoes the operation. That's why you were called here."

"Take me to her," Nancy said.

The nurse led the way down the silent corridor. Opening the door to Miss Chapelle's room, she motioned for Nancy to enter.

CHAPTER IX

THE MESSAGE IN THE HOLLOW OAK

NANCY moved quietly to the bedside of the injured authoress. A faint smile flickered over Miss Chapelle's wan face as she recognized the girl.

"Please—leave us alone," she murmured to the nurse on duty.

The attendant nodded and went out, closing the door softly behind her.

"I sent for you because there is something I have to tell you," Miss Chapelle began with difficulty. "The chances are that I shall never survive this operation."

Nancy tried to say something encouraging, but the authoress scarcely paid any attention to the girl's words.

"If anything should happen to me—will you promise to deliver a message to my grandfather? And to someone else whom I love dearly?"

"Of course, but I feel sure there will be no need for it. You will recover in a little while and be able to take the message yourself."

Miss Chapelle shook her head sadly.

"I fear that I shall never see my beloved Canada again."

"Canada?" Nancy questioned. "But I thought your home was in Hollywood."

"For years it has been. However, I was born in Canada. My real name is Annette Chap, although few people know it. My parents died when I was only six years old. Until I was sixteen I made my home with my grandfather, Pierre Chap."

"And is he still living in Canada?" Nancy probed gently.

"I have not heard any news of him in many years. I do know that if he is still living, he makes his home in the same log cabin. It is fifteen miles from Lake Wellington, deep in the woods. Anyone can direct you there."

"If he is still alive, I'll find him," Nancy promised.

A faraway expression crept into Annette Chap's misty gray eyes.

"Grandfather Pierre must be almost seventy years of age, but he has always been healthy and strong. How I should love to see him again!"

"You will, I feel sure."

"No, we are estranged. I ran away from home when I was only sixteen."

The woman lapsed into silence. Presently she continued, speaking with increasing difficulty:

"I was inclined to be a romantic youngster, and I fell in love with a young man named Norman Ranny."

Nancy started upon hearing the familiar surname, but the authoress did not notice her sudden movement.

"Grandfather thought I was too young to have boy friends," she went on. "He fairly hated Norman, and threatened to disown me if I were ever to marry him. But we were desperately in love. Finally, we decided to elope."

Miss Chap slumped back against the pillows, and for a time appeared too weak to continue her story. But she forced herself to go on.

"We agreed, Norman and I, to carry on a correspondence through the medium of the old oak tree."

"The hollow oak you mentioned before?" Nancy asked alertly.

"Yes. There was one more than a hundred years old. In its trunk was a hollow of which only Norman and I were aware. We used it as a hiding-place for our messages. I promised Norman that when I set the day for our elopement I would leave word for him in the hollow oak."

"And did you?"

"Yes, I wrote the message, saying I would meet him in a small town in the States just over the border. Grandfather Pierre kept such close watch over me that it was the only way to go about it.''

''And did Norman meet you?'' Nancy inquired gently. She had already inferred that the plans had not been carried out.

''No,'' Miss Chap returned, a strained look coming over her face. ''I stayed at the town for two days, but he failed to appear. After that I was afraid to return to my grandfather. No doubt I made a great mistake, but I was very proud. When Norman failed to come I felt I could never bear facing him again.''

''Perhaps he did not receive the message,'' Nancy suggested.

''I thought of that possibility later,'' Miss Chap confessed. ''At any rate, thereafter I went to Hollywood. I had a very hard time for many years, until success finally came to me almost over night. Now I have plenty of money. When I met you on the train I was on my way back to Canada to find my grandfather, and beg his forgiveness.''

''Have you heard from Norman since you left your home?''

''Only indirectly. I have been told that he is still unmarried. I know that he served in the World War, but I have no idea where he is living at present. I should like to see him again, but I fear that will never be.''

''Don't feel so discouraged,'' Nancy urged. ''The operation will surely be successful.''

"I hope so," Miss Chap said, smiling faintly. "But I have no real hope, so that's why I sent for you. The story I have just told you has been incorporated in my new novel. It is the best work I have ever done, for it is in reality the story of my life. If somehow you can find my old grandfather and tell him the truth about me before he dies, I shall be eternally grateful to you."

"I gladly accept the trust," Nancy promised seriously.

Miss Chap relaxed slightly.

"Now I shall rest easier. You have been very kind."

The door suddenly opened and a nurse came in.

"I'm sorry, but you'll have to leave now," she said to Nancy. "It is time to take Miss Chapelle to the operating room."

A slight shudder passed through the authoress as she realized that the ordeal was so near at hand. But she smiled bravely as Nancy bent down to kiss her.

"Keep up your courage," the girl whispered, a warm smile on her face.

She remained in the hall until she saw the attendants wheel the white-robed figure toward the operating room. After that she waited in the lobby. Some time later a nurse came in to inform her that the operation had been performed.

"Will she live?" Nancy asked tensely.

"She has a fair chance," was the response. "We will call you at your hotel as soon as Miss Chapelle comes out of the anaesthetic."

After she left the hospital Nancy did not return immediately to the Hamilton Hotel. Instead, she telephoned to Bess and George, and asked them to meet her at the Ranny farm.

"We'll get there as soon as we can," George promised. "But why are you in such a hurry?"

Nancy said she would explain everything later. She was waiting at the lane which led to the farm cottage when the girls drove up in a rented car.

"I'd have returned to the hotel for you, but time was so very short," Nancy apologized. "Miss Chapelle told me her true name as well as the sad story of her life. I think I have a clue as to what became of her former sweetheart. By the time she comes out of ether I hope to have some good news for her."

"You're talking in absolute riddles," Bess announced, as the three hurried toward the house on the hill.

"I suppose I am," Nancy admitted, laughing. "I'm so excited that my thoughts are going around in a fearful whirl. Oh, if I only could find Norman, how wonderful that would be!"

"Norman?" George demanded.

"Norman Ranny. I have a hunch that he may perhaps be related to these Rannys!"

As the girls walked up the winding lane, Nancy told her chums the main facts of Miss Chapelle's story. Bess and George grew excited.

"After all that occurred here as a result of our bringing Mrs. Donnelly, we may not be received very well," Bess remarked uneasily.

"I think Mrs. Ranny will talk to us," Nancy insisted. "It wasn't our fault that she and Mrs. Donnelly were involved in a feud."

The farm woman did not bear the girls any ill-will. When they knocked at her door she bade them enter in as cordial a manner as ever.

"I know why you have come," she said before Nancy could speak. "It is kind of you to offer to help patch up the trouble between Mrs. Donnelly and myself, but that is quite impossible."

"I have come on an entirely different mission," Nancy told the woman. "I should like to know if by any chance you have a son named Norman?"

A queer expression flickered over Mrs. Ranny's face.

"Yes, I have."

Nancy was elated.

"Then tell me where I can find him," she pleaded. "I must see him at once!"

"I don't know where he is."

CHAPTER X

"I DON'T know where my son is just at present," Mrs. Ranny repeated reluctantly.

"Have you any idea when he will return home!" Nancy questioned eagerly.

"No, he often goes and comes without explaining his whereabouts to me. Since he was in the war Norman has changed so that we hardly know him as the same person he used to be."

"Did he ever marry?"

"His sweetheart disappointed him, and he never fully recovered from the shock."

By this time Nancy was almost convinced that the Norman whom she was seeking was none other than Mrs. Ranny's son. She longed to tell the woman the entire story, yet hesitated to do so, for the secret was not hers to divulge. It would be best, she decided, to make a quiet investigation before revealing what she had learned.

"Could you furnish me with a picture of your son?" she next inquired of Mrs. Ranny. "Preferably one taken before he went to war?"

By this time Mrs. Ranny had become somewhat alarmed. She could not figure out what lay behind the questions.

"Yes, I believe I have an old picture of him," she agreed a trifle unwillingly. "Wait, and I'll go look."

She went over to a desk, and after rummaging through several drawers found an old faded photograph which she gave to Nancy.

"It's not a very good likeness of him," she said apologetically.

The face which Nancy saw was not strictly handsome, but the well-defined features denoted strength of character.

"This should serve my purpose very nicely," the girl announced.

Mrs. Ranny looked troubled.

"You didn't want to keep the picture?"

"Why, yes, may I, just for a few days? I promise to return it to you uninjured."

Obviously, Mrs. Ranny did not wish to lend her the photograph. However, she could think of no graceful way in which to refuse. While the woman was still debating the matter, Nancy thanked her again, and with the picture in her possession hurried away.

"Poor woman, you frightened her almost to death," Bess remarked, as they sped back to the hotel.

"She was afraid her son had done something dreadful."

Nancy had not considered this angle.

"I didn't want to worry her," she returned, "but I just had to get that picture. She'll probably not give the matter much thought."

In this Nancy was mistaken, however. She had no sooner left the house than Mrs. Ranny hurried to the barn to find her husband. The farmer, excitable by nature, was even more distressed than was his wife when he learned of Nancy's strange request for his son's picture. He feared that Norman had committed some crime, and that the photograph was to be used to identify him with the act.

All that afternoon the couple worried over the matter, until they finally convinced themselves that their son was wanted by the police. At length Mrs. Ranny proposed that they drive to town and ask Nancy point-blank what she intended to do with the photograph.

Meanwhile, unaware that she was causing the couple so much worry, Nancy returned with her chum to the Hamilton Hotel, where they found Mrs. Donnelly considerably improved. She was rocking restlessly in her chair as they came into her bedroom.

"I've been thinking that we may as well continue on to Wellington Lake," she announced abruptly. "I don't like this place, and I'm eager to get home. I'll convalesce there a lot faster than I will here."

"But are you really able to travel?" Nancy asked solicitously.

"Fiddlesticks! Of course I am. Seeing that Ranny woman upset me a little, I admit, but aside from that I'm as well as I ever was!"

Nancy smiled at this contradictory speech, for Mrs. Donnelly had not yet fully recovered from her injuries. However, the girls felt that once the woman made up her mind to travel, nothing would keep her from it.

Nancy thought it best not to tell Mrs. Donnelly the story Miss Chapelle had related to her at the hospital, since it concerned the Rannys. Secretly, she was eager to arrive at Wellington Lake as soon as possible so that she might fulfill the promise she had made to the authoress.

"I believe we can get a fast train out of here in about an hour," she said.

"Then have your luggage ready," the old lady advised crisply. "I packed my bag over an hour ago. I am sick and tired of this hotel, and we can't leave it any too soon to suit me!"

Elated at the thought of continuing on to Wellington Lake, Nancy hustled about making all necessary arrangements. Mrs. Donnelly went by automobile to the railroad station.

As they were boarding the train which was to take them North, Nancy noticed an old machine coming toward the tracks. It did not occur to her that the occupants, Mr. and Mrs. Ranny, were hastening to the station to talk to her.

After the train was well under way, Nancy saw to it that Mrs. Donnelly was comfortably settled in her berth, which had been made up early. Then with her chums she retired to the observation car to read a magazine.

"I wonder how Miss Chapelle is getting along?" Bess meditated. "It was too bad we didn't have another chance to see her before we left."

"Yes," Nancy agreed, "but the nurse told me that after the operation she would be unable to have visitors for several days. I feel that I can help her best by going on to Wellington Lake."

Learning that the train was scheduled to make a lengthy stop in half an hour at a junction, the girls discussed the possibility of telephoning long-distance to the hospital, and inquiring about Miss Chapelle's condition.

They were informed that they would have sufficient time in which to do this, so Nancy and her chums left the train at Valley Junction, Canada, and were soon in direct communication with the authorities at the Good Hope Hospital.

Great indeed was their joy to learn that the authoress had rallied after the operation, and was now resting easily.

"With that worry off my mind I'll be able to enjoy the trip North," Nancy said in relief as she and her chums swung aboard the train again. "Just think! In the morning we shall arrive at Wellington Lake!"

Until the last gleam of daylight remained, the girls sat out on the observation car platform admiring the rugged scenery. The hillsides along the tracks were thick with jackpine. The fragrant air was steadily growing cooler.

"Time to turn in," George suggested as the hour grew late.

"I'm as drowsy as an old tabby cat," Bess yawned. "It must be the change of air."

The cousins arose to go to their berths. Nancy, however, lingered behind.

"I'll be along in a minute or two," she promised.

For almost an hour she remained alone on the observation platform listening to the monotonous click of the wheels over the rails. She felt thrilled and excited. Lake Wellington! What a magic sound!

"I'll be there tomorrow," she told herself over and over. "Perhaps I'm foolish, but I can't help but feel that besides aiding Miss Chapelle, I'm to have a glorious vacation as well!"

At eight o'clock the following morning Nancy was re-strapping her bag, when George burst into the dressing room to tell her that the train was rapidly approaching their destination.

"I'm all ready, George. I'll be with you in an instant."

Ten minutes later the train pulled into Wellington Lake, and a porter aided the party to alight. Mrs. Donnelly had telegraphed ahead that she was coming, so a car was waiting to take them all to her boarding house.

"Well, girls, what do you think of the country?" she asked cheerfully when they were seated in the conveyance. "Pretty, isn't it?"

"The town of Wellington Lake is beautiful," Nancy told her truthfully. "I love the smell of the pines."

"We're coming to the water now," the old lady announced as they rounded a bend in the road. "Did you ever see any so blue?"

"Never!" Bess gasped, surveying the lake in awe.

"The fishing is good here, too," Mrs. Donnelly went on proudly. "Toss in a hook almost anywhere, and you'll catch perch or pike. Plenty of trout, too."

"I believe I'll have very little time in which to fish," Nancy said doubtfully. "I want to look over my property, and I also must visit some people who live about fifteen miles from here."

Mrs. Donnelly looked up alertly, but it was not in her nature to ask questions.

"If you go into the woods you'll need a guide," she advised. "This is rough country, and the farther you get from Lake Wellington the rougher it becomes.''

The woman's boarding house deserved a more elegant name. The place consisted of a large building made of logs, which nestled in a setting of tall pines. The interior was comfortably furnished. Glowing embers smoldered in a great open fireplace.

A woman whom Mrs. Donnelly termed the ''hired girl'' had breakfast waiting for them.

''I don't wonder you were eager to get here,'' Nancy smiled, taking a third helping of pancakes. ''The food is delicious.''

''You're nibbling at those flapjacks like a little bird! Wait until you've been here a week—then you'll eat hearty!''

''I thought I was doing remarkably well,'' Nancy laughed.

''Wait until I get into a kitchen apron,'' Mrs. Donnelly threatened, lowering her voice lest the ''hired girl'' hear. ''I'll cook up some real messes!''

''You mustn't overdo,'' Bess warned her. ''Remember, you were in bed only yesterday.''

''Fiddlesticks! I feel as good now as I ever did.''

After breakfast Bess and George went directly to their rooms. Nancy, however, had glimpsed a local paper on the living room table, and lingered to glance over it. The news was of a trivial nature, though interesting. Suddenly she caught sight of a familiar name, and eagerly read every word of the item. It told of a bad wind storm which had struck the district directly north of Wellington Lake. A stranger seated under a huge old oak tree on the Pierre Chap property had narrowly escaped death when a large bough had been snapped off.

"I wonder if that could be the tree Miss Chapelle told me about!" Nancy asked of herself excitedly. "The old 'letter-box' oak! Early tomorrow I shall go there."

CHAPTER XI

Into the Woods

THE next morning at breakfast Nancy spoke of her desire to visit the Chap property. She was relieved when Mrs. Donnelly offered some practical advice without asking leading questions.

"Pete Atkins is one of the best guides in this part of the country. For a very reasonable sum he'll furnish you with a boat and all necessary equipment, as well as cook your lunch for you."

"Must we go by boat?" Nancy questioned in surprise.

"That would be the only sensible way. The Chap property has a corduroy road leading up to it, but I know you would find the route tedious. By boat you will have a far more enjoyable time."

"I think the water trip would be lots of fun," George remarked.

"Well, hardly that," Mrs. Donnelly smiled, "for you must make two portages between lakes. However, it will be a worthwhile experience."

"How can we get in touch with Pete Atkins?" Nancy inquired.

"I'll make all arrangements for you if you wish. When would you want to start?"

"As soon as possible."

Mrs. Donnelly glanced at the clock.

"It is late now, but if Pete works fast you might get away by nine o'clock. That should give you ample time to reach your destination before nightfall."

"Then we'll not return until tomorow," Nancy told her. "I won't know how long I'll be detained until after I get there."

"I'll not worry about your safety as long as Pete Atkins looks after you," Mrs. Donnelly assured her.

Arrangements were soon completed, and the girls went to their rooms to dress for the trip. When the guide met them at the boat landing, he nodded approvingly as he saw that they wore riding breeches and knee-high shoes.

"Take good care of my girls," Mrs. Donnelly cautioned him.

"The best ever," he grinned.

Pete had brought along a small "kicker" motor. As the little boat shot across the lake the girls thought that the journey was to be both a rapid and a pleasant one. They soon arrived at the first portage, and there the motor was left behind.

"We'll carry only paddles and the grub,"

Pete explained as they set off through a narrow forest trail. "I have a canoe hidden at Lake Stewart."

Each of the girls had a light pack to transport. Before they had gone a mile, however, their burdens seemed to have taken on at least twenty pounds additional weight. They were overjoyed and relieved when they came within view of sparkling blue water again.

Pete drew out a red canoe from the bushes, where it had been cleverly hidden. Bending over to launch it, he gazed with interest at a fresh footprint in the sand.

"Someone's been through here this morning," he observed briefly. "City fellow, too."

"How can you tell?" Bess whispered curiously.

"Type of shoe," Nancy answered.

Pete helped the girls into the boat, and did not refer again to the footprint. However, as she sat in the bow helping to paddle, Nancy wondered idly who could have preceded them on the lake.

Her thoughts turned to Grandfather Chap. Would she find him at home and in good health? How disappointing it would be if she were to fail in her mission!

As she suddenly scanned the dazzling waters she observed a small moving object directly ahead. It was a boat. She pointed out the craft to the guide, but his sharp eyes had noted it long before she had. They dipped their paddles deeper, and gradually drew closer to the boat.

"It looks to me as if they're trying to keep well ahead of us," Nancy commented, a trifle puzzled.

Two men were in the canoe. Both of them handled their oars awkwardly. Nancy did not expect to recognize either of them, and therefore was greatly surprised when one of them glanced back and she caught a glimpse of his face.

"Why, it's Tom Stripe, I do believe!" she exclaimed.

The guide's face was as black as a thunder cloud.

"Do you know him?" Nancy demanded.

"He's been up here before," Pete snapped. "A yellow dog, if there ever was one!"

Nancy watched the boat closely. Unless she was greatly mistaken, Stripe's companion was none other than Raymond Niles! Had the two men purposely trailed her to Wellington Lake? She was afraid that trouble lay ahead of her.

The two men were aware that they had been seen, and accordingly took to their oars with a will. Soon they had disappeared behind a bend in the lake, where they were hidden from view. When Nancy and her party reached the spot a few minutes later, they saw no sign of the other boat.

"That's queer," she murmured. "I wonder where those men could have gone!"

Her eyes swept the shoreline, but the canoe was nowhere to be seen. However, it would be a very simple matter to conceal the craft among the dense bushes and pine trees that lined the water.

"Perhaps Niles and Stripe came up here only to fish," Bess observed optimistically. "Mrs. Donnelly told me this is one of the best fishing places in Canada."

"They won't get much of a catch by hiding in the bushes," the guide returned grimly.

Although Nancy and her chums surveyed the lake at intervals, they did not again catch sight of the two men. After an uneventful hour had passed they relaxed slightly.

"I'm hungry as a bear," George presently remarked.

The loyal guide smilingly pointed the canoe toward shore.

"We may as well stop for lunch. This is as good a place as any."

They pulled the craft up into the sandy beach and unloaded their knapsacks. The girls looked on admiringly as Pete built a fire. Then he took out a battered coffee pot and a smoke-blackened skillet. Soon the air was fragrant with the odor of bacon and potatoes frying.

The girls were ashamed of the amount of food they were able to consume. At home they might have scorned such simple fare, but after the morning's paddle even coarse bread tasted delicious.

"I'll go to the spring for some fresh water, and then we'll start on again," Pete announced after they had finished.

Nancy and her chums were clearing away the refuse, when they were startled at hearing a slight noise in the bushes.

"Who's there?" Nancy called out sharply.

Tom Stripe and Raymond Niles stepped out into the open.

"What do you want?" Nancy demanded.

"Oh, just a little talk with you," the latter said blandly. "We're interested in that newly-acquired property of yours."

"So I suspected!"

"Now don't get up on your high-horses," Niles wheedled. "We're not trying to cheat you out of anything."

"I wish I could be sure of that."

"We're perfectly willing to pay you a good price for your land."

"What price?" Nancy questioned shrewdly.

"The land cost you nothing, so anything you might make is clear profit. Now the property is barren—practically valueless. It will cost you more in taxes than it is worth. Considering all this, we feel that two hundred dollars would be more than a fair sum."

Nancy could not repress a smile.

"If the land is so worthless, why do you wish to acquire it!"

Niles had anticipated this question.

"It is located not far from a good fishing lake. We expect to erect a cabin there."

"I don't care to sell," Nancy said coldly.

"You're making a mistake," Tom Stripe snarled.

"I think I'm not!" Nancy retorted, angered by the surly tones. "If you must know the truth, I distrust both of you!"

"We want the land, and we'll get it, too!" Stripe fairly shouted. "If you won't sell to us, we'll strand you here! We'll wreck your canoe!"

In sudden rage he darted toward the shore where the craft had been left. Nancy and her chums pursued him, but Raymond Niles blocked their way. Stripe pushed the light canoe out into the water, and overturned it.

"Pete! Help!" Nancy shouted frantically.

Their guide came running down the trail. With one leap he was upon Tom Stripe.

The men struggled knee deep in water. Then, with a mightly blow, Pete struck the man under the chin. He reeled backward, lost his balance, and toppled over into the water.

Nancy had not remained idle. Raymond Niles held her arms, but she struggled valiantly to free herself. Just as Stripe pitched backwards she jerked away, taking her captor completely by surprise. Then she gave him a powerful shove. He stumbled and tried to save himself, but failed. With a yell of rage he, too, fell into the water.

For an instant Nancy stood watching the two men as they struggled to regain their footing. Then it dawned upon her that she and her friends were missing a golden opportunity to make their get-away.

"Quick!" she shouted to her companions. "Help me right the canoe!"

CHAPTER XII

THE OVERTURNED CANOE

BESS and George were too startled to obey, but Pete splashed out into the lake to help Nancy recover the floating craft. With a deft movement they flipped out most of the water from the canoe.

By this time the cousins had caught up the knapsacks, and now jumped into the boat which Pete steadied for them to get in. As soon as Nancy was in, he took his own place at the stern. Three mighty sweeps of the paddle, and the four were well beyond reach of Niles and Stripe, who stood neck-deep in water, glaring after the escaping party.

"I'll get even with you for this!" the latter shouted, shaking his fist.

"If I ever see you again, I'll give you a worse ducking!" Pete called back.

Niles gazed after the canoe ruefully, but there was an admiring look in his eyes as they rested upon Nancy Drew. He was forced to acknowledge her pluck. And she was certainly very pretty!

With the craft rapidly drawing farther and farther from shore, pursuit was out of the question. The bedraggled men gloomily betook themselves to their abandoned campfire, where they piled the wood high, and tried to dry their wet clothes.

As he was looking around for additional logs, Tom Stripe noticed a slip of paper lying on the ground. Curiously he picked it up. His face brightened at sight of it, for it was a notation which Nancy unwittingly had dropped during her scuffle with Niles.

The paper gave complete instructions for reaching the Chap homestead.

"We're in luck after all!" he said to his companion excitedly. "Nancy Drew wasn't so smart when she dropped this."

"Let's see it," Niles commanded.

His eyes gleamed as he read the directions.

"It's a dead give-away as to where she's going, Tom."

"Sure, and if we could just beat her there."

"They have the head start. That Pete Atkins paddles with the precision of a machine!"

"I hate him!" Stripe growled. "When I meet him again I'll fix him for throwing me into the lake!"

"Forget your grudge and do a little thinking. How are we going to get to old man Chap's before Nancy Drew?"

Stripe's eyes narrowed.

"I know a trail that leads there, but it's hard going."

"Let's try it anyway. We have no chance by water. I'll stand a lot of punishment in order to get the best of Nancy Drew!"

Without waiting for their clothing to dry thoroughly the two men set off through the woods. Stripe had not exaggerated when he said that the trail would be difficult. It was overgrown with vines and brush, so that in many places they bogged down nearly to their knees. Intent upon their purpose, they kept doggedly on their way.

"I'm getting good and sick of all this!" Niles announced in disgust after several hours of steady tramping. "It seems we should be getting there pretty soon. Tom, are you sure you know where we're going?"

"I thought I did. We may have taken the wrong fork back there a mile or so."

Niles glared at his companion as he wiped the perspiration from his grimy face.

"This is a fine time to decide you've made a mistake! I might have known you'd get me into a mess like this. We're in a fine pickle now! Lost in the wilderness, and not a living soul for miles around!"

"You're wrong about that, stranger," announced a voice from behind.

The men wheeled, to find themselves facing a bearded stranger who had quietly stepped out from among the bushes.

"Who are you?" Stripe demanded.

"Ranny is the name," the man informed him. "Norman Ranny."

Stripe and Niles had been quick to note that the newcomer carried prospecting tools.

"Is it true that there's gold around here?" Niles asked, a trifle tensely.

The man studied him coolly.

"Not here in the woods," he retorted.

"But along the streams?" Tom Stripe probed eagerly.

"Some say one thing, others say another," was the noncommittal reply.

"Could you give us a bite to eat and tell us how to get to old man Chap's place?" Niles questioned, realizing that it would do no good to ask about the gold. "We're hungry, and just about done up."

The prospector grew more friendly.

"You're not far from Pierre Chap's cabin now. If you want to come on to my place farther down the trail, I'll give you some food and show you the way."

"All right. Let's get going," Stripe urged. "We're eager to reach there."

"Why the hurry, stranger?" Norman Ranny inquired as he led the way down the trail. "Up here we try to take things as they come."

"Well, that isn't my way," Stripe responded stiffly. "If you won't point out the trail——"

"No need to be so quick on the trigger," the

prospector drawled. "I'll show you the route all right. Only I thought you both looked done up and needed a rest."

"We do," Niles admitted. "We're trying to beat another party to old man Chap's, and we've been legging it as fast as we could possibly go."

Norman Ranny digested this information in silence. A little later they came within sight of a tiny cabin located in a clearing. The prospector flung wide the door, and invited the men to enter.

"I'll fix something to eat," he offered. "It won't take me long."

The two sat down, and looked curiously about them. The shack was comfortably, though plainly furnished. The chairs and tables were substantial, home-made pieces of furniture. A pair of snowshoes and some animal skins decorated the bare walls. Over the bed there hung the portrait of a young girl.

"Nice looking dame," Niles commented familiarly.

Norman Ranny bent lower over the stove, and pretended that he had not heard what had been said.

"Queer sort, isn't he?" Niles muttered in an undertone to his companion, and Stripe nodded uneasily.

For want of anything else to do, Niles drew from his pocket the scrap of paper Nancy had dropped. After re-reading the directions, he carelessly tossed the note onto the table.

A minute later, in setting down a dish, Norman Ranny glanced at the paper. A name which Nancy had jotted down stood out and held his attention. He re-read it to make sure he was not mistaken.

"Annette Chap!"

The words seared his very brain! That was the name of his former sweetheart!

"What's the matter?" Niles demanded suddenly. "You look sick."

Ranny stared at him almost stupidly.

"Where did you get this paper?" he questioned.

"Oh, from a girl," Niles told him carelessly.

"A girl," Ranny repeated, as if in a daze.

Niles and Stripe exchanged glances. What was wrong with the man? He acted as if he were not quite sane.

"Say, I think we'll not wait for food," Stripe said, rising quickly to his feet. "If you'll point out the way to old man Chap's we'll not trouble you any longer."

"And all the while I thought her dead——" the prospector muttered. "Could it be I've made a mistake?"

"What was that?" Niles demanded, bewildered.

With an effort the prospector forced himself to become aware of the two men.

"I am very sorry," he apologized. "I'll have dinner ready in a few minutes."

"But we said—" Defeated, Stripe sank back once more into his chair.

"It's of no use," Niles warned his companion in a whisper. "He's out of his mind. We must humor him, or he may try to kill us."

The two crooks scarcely took their eyes off the man as he went on preparing the meal. Soon the food was ready. The men ate what the prospector set before them, but with little appetite.

Norman Ranny did not join them. He sat opposite the group, staring moodily into space. His attitude was depressing to his companions. When they had finished with their meal they arose in obvious relief.

"Many thanks," Niles said, a trifle too heartily to sound sincere. "Now, if you'll point out the trail, Mr. Ranny, we'll be on our way again."

The prospector also rose.

"I'll go with you," he said.

"There's no need for that," Stripe interposed hastily.

"We'll find our way easily," Niles added.

"The trail is winding. There are several forks."

"We've troubled you enough," Stripe insisted stubbornly.

He did not want the propector to accompany

them. Besides, it was not desirable to have a witness to their actions after they should have reached the Chap cabin.

"It seems to me you don't care for my company, stranger."

"Oh, no, it isn't that," Niles said quickly. "Of course we want you to go, but we don't like to put you to so much trouble."

"No trouble at all. Come along. I'll lead the way."

Thoroughly disgusted, Niles and Stripe reluctantly followed their host from the cabin. It was not until they had gone some distance along the trail that they recalled the scrap of paper. Niles could not remember having seen it lying on the table as they had left the shack.

He glanced curiously at their guide. Had Ranny picked it up? It did not seem at all probable, although the prospector's attitude had changed almost from the moment he had seen the handwriting. Shrugging his shoulders, Niles abandoned the problem.

"Maybe we can get away from him a little farther on," Stripe suggested in a whisper.

They waited hopefully for an opportunity to do so, but whenever they lingered on the trail Norman Ranny stopped until they caught up again.

"We can't shake him," Niles whispered irritably. "No use in trying."

Soon they came to a large clearing with a

small cabin surrounded by cultivated fields.
About three hundred yards from the house
there stood an old mill.

"Chap has a nice place here," the prospector said quietly. "He cleared all the land himself."

"Well, thanks for showing us the way,"
Stripe remarked significantly.

Norman Ranny made no move to depart.
"I may as well wait around here and see if
anyone is at home."

Infuriated, the two men stalked up to the
front door, and knocked loudly upon it.

CHAPTER XIII

A Ruse

There was no response. Niles knocked again at the door.

"I thought he wouldn't be here," Norman Ranny said.

He watched the two men closely, and they could not help but see the suspicious look in his eyes. Exasperated, Stripe flung open the door that had been left unlocked.

"Look here," Norman Ranny protested, following them inside. "You can't break into a man's house like this!"

"Oh, can't we?" Stripe sneered.

Wheeling about, he leaped upon the surprised man, and dropped him to the floor. Niles aided in holding the victim down until his arms and legs could be tied.

"Put a gag in his mouth, too," Stripe advised, "or he'll be letting out a yell at the wrong time!"

His companion found an old towel which he stuffed between the prospector's teeth.

"I guess that will keep him safe for a while," he observed in relief. "No telling what he might have done to us if he'd had the chance.''

''Chap may come back any minute,'' Stripe commented uneasily. ''We'll have to hide this fellow somewhere.''

Niles was peering into the dark basement.

''I think there's some sort of closet or fruit cellar down there,'' he said.

The two men carried the helpless prospector below, and locked him in the little stuffy room which Niles had discovered. Carefully they closed the entrance to the dungeon-like place and returned to the upper floor. Scarcely had they recovered their breaths than Niles, who was standing by the window, observed Nancy Drew and her party beaching their canoe on the lake shore.

''We were just in time, Tom. What's our next move?''

''We'll hide, and let them walk into our trap.''

No sooner had the two secreted themselves than a knock was heard upon the door. This was repeated several times.

Niles and Stripe waited breathlessly, expecting that Nancy and her friends would soon give up and force their way in. But the little party did not choose to intrude upon private property. Instead, Nancy gazed speculatively toward the old mill, which stood at some distance from the house.

"Mr. Chap may be working there," she suggested. "Shall we investigate?"

Not until she and her companions had reached the dilapidated old building did they see that it had not been used in recent years. The stream that fed the water wheel had entirely dried away.

"It isn't likely Mr. Chap is here," George commented.

"After walking this far we may as well make sure," Nancy said.

She led the way toward the structure. Bess and George, attracted by the water wheel, stopped to look at it, and Nancy, going on, presently lost sight of the guide, also. She wandered alone through the machinery room and examined the granary.

Impelled by some impulse which she could not explain, she walked over to the decaying wall. Stooping over, she peered through one of the large cracks, through which she could see the inside of the cabin quite plainly. Tom Stripe was standing at the window, cautiously peering out.

Nancy could hardly believe her eyes. However, a second glance assured her that she had not been mistaken. Stripe and Niles had arrived ahead of her at the shack. For all she knew, they might have harmed Grandfather Pierre!

Hastily she returned to her friends, and in

terse sentences reported to them what she had seen.

"They hope to take us by surprise," she said. "We must outwit them."

"But how?" George demanded.

In a few words Nancy outlined a plan. Bess and George were to circle to the rear of the cabin, being careful not to be seen. From the trees they were to watch Stripe and his companion.

"Pete and I will sneak back and hide the canoe."

"But I don't see what good that will do," Bess protested.

"Perhaps it will do no good. But I'm hoping that Niles and Stripe will notice that the craft is gone, and come to the conclusion that we left with it."

"That's an idea," George chuckled. "Come on, Bess. Better take off that bright hat of yours. It's too conspicuous."

Keeping themselves well hidden by the brush, Nancy and the guide stole down to the shore where they had beached the canoe. They directed a hasty glance toward the cabin to make sure their movements had not been observed, and then drew the boat far back into the brush. At the girl's instigation Pete thereupon obliterated the tracks leading to the hiding place, a precaution which Nancy did not forget to take.

The pair then moved on down the beach, making a wide circle back to the rear of the old home.

For a long time nothing happened, and Nancy felt herself growing discouraged.

"I guess it's of no use," she said in disgust.

"Wait!" the guide directed, pulling her back into the bushes.

The door of the cabin slowly opened, and Raymond Niles peered cautiously forth. He motioned to Stripe, and the two made their way stealthily down to the water front.

"Why, they've gone!" the former exclaimed, observing the place where the canoe had been beached.

"That's queer," his companion muttered, looking about him. "I didn't see them leave."

"I lost sight of them when they went into the old mill," Niles added. "Wonder where they could have gone?"

"Not back to Wellington Lake, that's certain. Nancy Drew wouldn't give up so easily."

"You're right," Niles agreed. "Say, I'll bet that guide of hers knows where to find Chap."

"Likely as not he's gone to inspect Nancy Drew's new property. It adjoins his land, and he may have decided to buy it."

"Say, why didn't we think of that before?"

Niles demanded. "I wondered why she was streaking it way off here. Must be she has some arrangement with Chap about buying the land."

"That's why she wouldn't deal with us," Stripe growled.

The two men peered out over the lake, but there was no sign of the little red canoe.

"If we only had a boat we might overtake them," Stripe muttered. "I know the location of the land."

They glanced up and down the shore. As chance would have it, Pierre Chap had left his boat beached upon the sand only a hundred yards away. With one accord the two men ran toward it.

"They'll get good and tired before they've rowed that tub very far," the girls' guide chuckled, as he saw the men launch the craft. "It weighs a ton, and Pierre Chap never uses it any more."

After the boat was far out upon the lake, Nancy and Pete joined George and Bess, who had witnessed everything from the rear of the cabin. They had climbed tall trees, and from their lookout had been able to see and hear clearly all that was going on.

"Pierre Chap should be coming home soon," Nancy said thoughtfully, as the party considered its next move. "Maybe we ought to go inside the cabin and see how things are."

"I'll stay outdoors and keep watch," Pete offered, opening the door for the girls to enter. "Stripe and his friend may decide to come back. It's better to have someone remain on guard."

Nancy and her chums settled themselves comfortably inside the homestead, being careful all the while to disturb nothing. Everything was in order; only the breakfast dishes had not been washed.

"At least we know that Mr. Chap has been here today," Nancy commented, "so it's quite likely that he'll return before dark."

After some time the girls grew tired of sitting around idle, so Bess suggested that they wash and dry the dishes.

"We may as well," George agreed. "It will help Mr. Chap, and at the same time keep us from dying of boredom."

Bess heated some water on the little oil stove, and soon had some clean dishes for her chums to dry. Nancy was putting them away in the cupboard when she abruptly halted, and listened intently.

"What's wrong?" George asked uneasily.

Nancy did not answer immediately.

"I guess it was nothing," she finally responded.

She did not want to disturb her chums, yet was positive that she had heard a queer noise coming from the cellar.

"You must be imagining things," Bess laughed. "There is something about this place that gets on one's nerves—it must be the silence."

"I didn't hear a thing," George added. "It must have been——"

Her words ended in a surprised gasp, for a low groan seemed to issue from the very floor boards. "Did you hear that?" she whispered apprehensively.

"What could it have been?" Bess shuddered.

"It sounded like someone in pain," Nancy replied.

They huddled together, listening intently. A moment later they heard the strange noise again—a loud, unearthly moan.

"It's a ghost," Bess insisted, her teeth chattering with fright.

"There are no ghosts," Nancy returned firmly. But it took all her courage to add, "I'm going down to the cellar and find out just what it really is!"

CHAPTER XIV

THE CELLAR GHOST

BESS and George tried to dissuade Nancy from descending into the dark basement.

"You don't know what might be down there," Bess whispered tensely. "So why risk your life!"

"I'll be all right," Nancy maintained. "If anything should happen, just step to the door and call Pete."

"Let's get him now," George urged.

"No, we need him out there to keep guard. I'm going to investigate this place myself."

Courageously, Nancy lifted the trap-door and peered down into the dark cellar. Despite her air of confidence, she did not enjoy the task she had assigned to herself.

"If I only had a light——"

She murmured the phrase as she slowly descended into the dark void. Bess and George, waiting fearfully at the top of the stairs, heard the words blur off. Their chum had vanished!

Suddenly there came a slight commotion from below. Bess and George huddled against the wall, fearing the worst. Before they had recovered from their fear, Nancy emerged, clutching a gray cat. Her young chums were so relieved when they saw what the trouble had been that they burst into laughter.

"Behold the ghost!" Nancy smiled.

"A cat!" George exclaimed contemptuously. She bent down to stroke the animal. "Nice Tabby, nice Tabby. Tell me, how did you learn to make such unearthly sounds?"

Nancy closed the trap-door. The animal seemed to be entirely satisfied with the new quarters. Ignoring the girls, the little creature went over to a warm corner, curled up, and was soon dozing.

"It's hard to believe that one small cat could cause so much excitement," Nancy smiled. "I'm glad we didn't call Pete, for he would have laughed at us."

Again the girls settled themselves to await the return of Pierre Chap. The clock on the mantel struck five and simultaneously with the last note, a loud moan issued from the cellar. Nancy and her chums jumped up from their chairs.

"*That* wasn't the cat," George whispered.

Bess gripped Nancy's arm, trembling with fright.

"I'll find out what it is," the Drew girl said determinedly.

Before she could move there was a loud

crash that seemed to come from under their very feet.

"Oh! Oh!" Bess wailed, and toppled over in a faint.

Nancy rushed to the door.

"Pete! Pete!" she called.

There was no response to her cry. The guide had vanished. She darted back into the house and helped George carry Bess out into the open air. There the girl quickly revived, although her face remained pale.

"Let's take the canoe and get away from here as soon as possible," she pleaded.

"We can't leave without Pete," Nancy told her.

The guide's strange disappearance troubled and annoyed her. Surely the man had not abandoned them deliberately!

Nancy glanced toward the horizon. The sun was still fairly high, but the woods were dark and gloomy. The thought of remaining at the Chap cabin after dark with no older person present caused even her courageous heart to quail.

For an instant she was tempted to heed Bess's suggestion, but put the thought from her mind. Even if they should start for Wellington Lake without delay, they could not hope to reach that place before dark. Without Pete to guide them they would be hopelessly lost.

Nancy stared grimly at the homestead. It

challenged her. George read the thought which ran through her friend's mind.

"Nancy Drew, don't you dare to think of going back into that dreadful place!"

"Listen!" Bess commanded.

The groaning had started again!

Resolutely Nancy walked into the house. With the greatest of reluctance George and Bess followed her, pleading with her not to attempt anything reckless.

"Wait for me at the head of the stairs," Nancy directed. "I'm going to make a thorough investigation."

Cautiously she descended the steps, one at a time. It was so dark she could scarcely see a foot ahead of her. She groped her way along the wall, listening intently all the while.

Suddenly she stepped on something long and snake-like. There was a startled meow as the girl stumbled over the object that lay in her path. She then pitched headlong upon the damp floor.

"Nancy! Nancy!" Bess screamed in terror from above.

"I'm all right," their chum called, getting to her feet a trifle shakily. "I only stumbled over another cat."

"Do be careful," George warned her friend anxiously.

Nancy scarcely heard what they said, for she was listening intently to what she thought was the sound of soft breathing. Next there came an almost inaudible moan, which seemed to issue from the direction of the fruit closet.

Gathering her courage, the girl tried the door, but it would not open. Groping about in the musty darkness, she located the key in the lock and turned it. Opening the door a crack, she peered inside. At first she saw nothing; then gradually she could make out the figure of a man lying on the floor.

"Girls!" she shouted excitedly. "Come here! I think poor Mr. Chap has been hurt!"

Bess and George dashed down the stairs to help her. They stared aghast as they beheld the bearded man lying trussed and gagged on the cold, hard floor.

"Get a knife to cut his bonds," Nancy urged.

George ran back to the kitchen for the article, while Nancy and Bess removed the gag from the man's mouth.

"We'll soon have you free," they encouraged the fellow.

George came with the knife, and the thongs were quickly severed.

"Can you walk?" Nancy questioned him anxiously, as they helped the fellow to his feet.

"I think so," he responded with an effort.

Supporting him on either side, the girls assisted him up the stairs and into the kitchen. As the circulation improved in his numb limbs, he was able to walk more freely.

"Water," he pleaded.

Bess ran to get it. After the man had drunk deeply he smiled gratefully at the girls.

"I feel better now," he said, relieved.

Nancy studied his face intently.

"You can't be Pierre Chap," she declared, "for you are far too young."

"I live some distance from here," the bearded prospector told her. "Two men stopped me on the trail and asked me the way to this place. I grew suspicious, and decided to come with them. They overpowered me and threw me into the cellar. If it hadn't been for your timely arrival I might have lain there and died."

"It must have been Tom Stripe and Raymond Niles who did it," Nancy surmised. "Can you describe your assailants?"

The prospector gave an accurate description of the two men.

"They ought to be arrested for such an outrage!" George cried indignantly. "When we return to Lake Wellington we'll report the matter to the police."

The prospector looked troubled.

"I'd rather you wouldn't," he said. "I couldn't appear in court against them. I'd prefer to even the score myself."

During the conversation Nancy had remained strangely quiet, though her chums noted that she stared at the stranger in a most peculiar manner. In truth, the Drew girl was bewildered. From the first the man had reminded her of someone, and vainly did she rack her memory. Where had she seen him before?

Suddenly the answer came to her. Save for the beard, the stranger put her in mind of a photograph she had in her possession. Trying not to show her excitement, she turned to the prospector and asked him eagerly: "Can it be possible that you are Norman Ranny?"

CHAPTER XV

THE stranger stared at Nancy in astonishment. For an instant she thought he intended to deny his identity, but he reluctantly nodded his head in assent.

"Yes, I am Norman Ranny. How did you know?"

"Your mother lent me your photograph," Nancy explained. "I also met Ann Chapelle, who told me her right name was Annette Chap."

The color drained from the man's face at mention of his former sweetheart.

"You have seen Annette?" he demanded, gripping Nancy's arm so tightly that it hurt her. "Then she is still alive?"

"Yes. When I last heard from the hospital she was slowly improving. She was seriously injured in a train wreck a while back and for some time the doctors feared she could not live. Even now she is not entirely out of danger."

"My poor Annette! If only I might go to her!"

"Can't you?" Nancy asked quietly.

"I am afraid she would not care to see me."

"I firmly believe she still loves you," Nancy assured him.

Norman Ranny hung upon the girl's words, though he shook his head sadly.

"I should like to think so, but unfortunately I am unable to."

"Why do you say that?" Nancy inquired, puzzled at his attitude. "Surely it cannot be that you've changed in your feelings toward Miss Chap."

A trifle uneasily she recalled the story the authoress had told her concerning the message in the hollow oak. If it were true that Norman Ranny had ignored the note, it was possible that even now he desired to avoid the entangling fetters of matrimony.

"I haven't changed in my regard for Annette," the man told her sincerely. "I have always loved her, and I always will."

"Then why can't you go to her now?"

"You don't understand. I have nothing to offer her. I am only a prospector—why, people in this community do not even know my real name. I thought it best to change it after I returned from the war."

"You have lived here ever since?" Nancy inquired.

"No. I visit my parents occasionally, and have stayed in many states and countries. There's something about this community that always draws me back. I guess it's because I knew Annette here."

Nancy nodded understandingly. Then the man went on, speaking brusquely to hide his emotions:

"When I was discharged from the Army I was told that Annette had died. Until today I had no suspicion that she might still be alive."

"Tell me, do you ever visit the old hollow oak?" Nancy asked significantly.

"Yes, quite often. I was almost killed there two nights ago during a terrific wind storm. While I was sitting under the tree, a large bough snapped off."

"Then you were the stranger mentioned in the newspaper," Nancy commented.

"Yes. Here is the proof of it," the man smiled, pushing back his hair to reveal a deep gash in his scalp. "It was a wonder I wasn't killed. Not that it would have mattered greatly."

"Oh, you mustn't talk that way," Nancy said hastily.

"I can't help feeling the way I do. Life has never been worth while since I lost Annette."

"But wasn't it your own fault?" Nancy inquired gently.

"My own fault? What do you mean?"

"Didn't you ignore the message she left for you in the oak tree?"

Norman Ranny laughed shortly.

"I have been trying to forget it all my life."

"But why did you never meet her as she requested?" Nancy asked, a trifle exasperated.

"Meet her? The note said nothing about that."

"Didn't it state the town just over the border where she expected to join you?"

"It most certainly did not. Annette wrote me a very cold note. I recall the words. She said, 'I will not elope. I would rather have my grandfather's money.'"

"That isn't the way she explained it to me," Nancy gasped. "It must all have been a hoax! Perhaps someone changed the messages."

She then recounted everything Miss Chapelle had told her in the hospital, noting all the while that Norman Ranny was deeply moved by the story.

"I can't understand it," he murmured after she had finished. "If I thought she was still waiting for me I'd go to her at once."

"I'm sure she is," Nancy told him.

"She wrote the note nearly nineteen years ago, and I know we have both changed greatly since that time. You tell me that Annette is now a successful novelist. But I have so little to offer her."

Nancy tried to persuade him that he was sufficient unto himself. Though he listened closely to her words, they seemed to make no definite impression upon him.

"Had I known about the exchange of notes before I went to war, everything might have been different now," he said sadly. "Annette has her place in the city and I have my work here in the woods."

"But if you knew that she needed you?" Nancy persisted.

"I'd drop everything and go to her."

After a moment's silence Nancy questioned:

"Do you often see Grandfather Chap?"

"Yes, though he does not know who I am. He became a recluse after his daughter ran away. He always ruled Annette with an iron hand, though he loved her dearly. Now he shuts himself up in his cabin with only his pet cats to keep him company."

"I've already met two of them," Nancy smiled, ruefully surveying a bruised elbow. "Have you any idea when Mr. Chap will return?"

"Not the slightest. It begins to look as if he doesn't intend to come back here tonight."

Nancy and her chums looked troubled.

"We don't know what to do," George confessed. "Our guide has disappeared. We're stranded here in the woods."

"Who is your guide?"

"Pete Atkins."

"That's queer. He's as reliable a man as you'll find in these parts."

"We don't know what to make of it," Nancy

admitted. "We brought along camping equipment, but it's very meager."

"The nights are pretty cold here," Norman Ranny warned. "If Mr. Chap or your guide should not return soon, I could take you to the nearest town where you might find more comfortable quarters."

The girls thanked him, and sat down to wait. The sun dropped lower in the sky. Long shadows soon fell upon the lake. In a short while it would be dusk.

"I doubt if it will do us any good to stay here much longer," Ranny suggested.

"I suppose we should be starting out," Nancy said.

After leaving a note for the guide in the event of his returning, Nancy and her chums followed the prospector a short distance through the dense timber until they arrived at a swiftly moving stream. From among the overhanging bushes the man drew forth a sturdy boat.

"This will be the quickest route," he stated, as he assisted the girls into the craft.

Nancy was reluctant to leave the vicinity, for she had not had a chance either to talk to Pierre Chap or to inspect her newly-acquired property. As they rowed down the stream, skillfully avoiding rocks and boulders, she drew the prospector into conversation concerning the mineral value of neighboring land. When Norman Ranny replied to her questions and displayed an interest in her affairs, she gave him a description of the tract she owned.

"It's not far from here," the prospector told her, "though it is in an even wilder section than this. Too bad you couldn't have inspected it."

"That's what I really wanted to do," Nancy admitted. "It's disappointing to have to leave without having seen it."

Ranny rested on his oars as he debated the situation.

"Well, why not turn around and go back?" he proposed. "I know a trapper and his wife with whom you might perhaps spend the night. In the morning you could continue on to your own property."

"Let's do it!" George declared enthusiastically. "After all, we made the trip to Canada partly in a spirit of adventure!"

"Mrs. Donnelly won't worry about us if we don't get back to Wellington Lake for several days," Bess added.

Nancy required no urging to decide in favor of the trip, and gratefully accepted the prospector's generous offer to take them to the Dawson cabin. Norman Ranny directed the boat into a side stream, which was even swifter than the one they had previously taken. It required all his skill to keep them from being dashed against the rocks. Now and then a low-hanging bush would swish against the girl's cheeks, cutting like a whip.

"I can hardly wait until I see the land," Nancy declared excitedly. "How thrilled I'd be if there were gold on it!"

"That is the sustaining hope of every prospector," Ranny smiled. "But this property of yours sounds mighty good to me. I've found several big nuggets in Pebble Creek, which flows through your place."

"I'd love to see a nugget," Bess remarked.

Resting on his oars for a moment, Ranny took a small leather bag from his pocket and offered it to her. Somewhat awed, Bess withdrew several small lumps of gold, balancing them in the palm of her hand.

"I thought they would glitter more than this," she said.

Ranny laughed.

"They may not look like gold to you now," he said, "but they are, just the same."

After each of the girls had finished examining the specimens, Bess returned the bag to the prospector.

"I hope we'll find a few nuggets on my property," Nancy said wistfully. "I'd like to take them home with me as souvenirs."

"I'll help you pan the stream if we have time," Ranny offered.

It was quite dark when the man finally guided the boat into a cove, and moored it. Through the trees the girls could see a light burning in a cabin. Ranny led the way, and in response to his knock a woman came to the door. She greeted him warmly, calling him by a name that was unfamiliar to Nancy and her chums.

"Come right in," she said, when she saw the girls. "We don't have many visitors, and we're always glad to entertain them."

The evening meal was cooking on a stove. The delightful aroma nearly overpowered Nancy and her chums, for they were weak from hunger.

"Sit in," Mr. Dawson, the trapper, invited cordially, drawing up chairs for the girls. "The food's plain, but there's plenty of it."

Again the three chums were ashamed of their hearty appetites, though Mr. and Mrs. Dawson insisted that they were not doing full justice to the various dishes offered them. When Nancy tactfully suggested that she intended to pay for all the trouble she and her friends were causing, the couple refused to listen.

"Don't you give it a second thought," their hostess chuckled. "It's a treat for us to have you here."

In truth, the kindly people seemed to be enjoying the company of the girls, and plied them with innumerable questions about city life. After the supper dishes had been washed, the trapper brought out his banjo and played several gay, old-fashioned tunes.

"Our sons should be coming in before long," Mrs. Dawson told Nancy. "Herman went to the nearest settlement for our monthly order of groceries. Jake, the older boy, started out to do some trout fishing."

As she spoke, the woman crossed over to the window to peer out. It troubled her that her boys had not yet returned.

"I can't understand what's keeping Jake," she remarked a little later. "It's too dark for him to be fishing now."

Ten minutes later footsteps could be heard outside. The door was flung open, and a youth, clad in the rough garments of a woodsman, staggered into the room, bending low under the weight of a man whom he carried on his back.

"Jake!" Mrs. Dawson cried, rushing to him. "What has happened?"

"I found him on the trail," he told his mother breathlessly, lowering the fellow to a couch. "He's badly hurt."

Nancy glanced anxiously at the injured man. He was Pete Atkins!

CHAPTER XVI

A False Claim

THE guide stirred restlessly upon the couch as Nancy bent over him.

"Tom Stripe did it," he mumbled. "I'll get even!"

Mrs. Dawson ran for a basin of warm water with which to sponge a gash on the victim's neck. A large bump stood out upon the back of Pete's head, and Nancy suspected that the man had been struck from behind with a heavy club.

"I don't believe he's as badly hurt as it appeared at first," Norman Ranny said after they had worked over Pete for some time. "If he gets a good sleep he should be all right in the morning."

"If he isn't, I'll start for a doctor," Jake offered.

Nancy and her friends were given a room for the night. Ranny and Jake, who did not mind sleeping in the open, rolled up in blankets in the back yard. It was thought best not to move the guide from the couch, so Mr. Dawson spent the night watching by his bedside.

In the morning Pete was considerably improved, though in no condition to endure the hardships of the trail. When Nancy questioned him as to what had transpired, he offered but little information.

"Tom Stripe and I have an old grudge. He got me this time, but wait until we meet again!" was all he would say.

Although Nancy disliked leaving Pete behind, she realized he could hope for no better care than at the hands of the kindly Mrs. Dawson. It seemed best that the girl go forward with her plans for viewing the newly-acquired tract of land. Mr. Dawson furnished the party with excellent saddle horses, and his wife packed a lunch for the girls to take with them.

"You'll be perfectly safe with your new guide," she assured Nancy, smiling in Norman Ranny's direction. "There isn't a better woodsman in this part of the country than he."

Leaving the Dawson cabin, the party rode single file along a steep, rocky trail. Often their course would lead them beside some winding stream, where they paused to permit their horses to drink.

"Did you ever see such marvelous scenery before in all your life?" Bess demanded admiringly, as they paused at the crest of a pine knoll to gaze back toward the Dawson cabin. "Aren't you the lucky girl, Nancy, to own property in such a gorgeous district as this?"

"I'll not be very lucky if there isn't any gold

here," Nancy laughed. "The land is so in-accessible for me it would be worthless for any other purpose."

At noon they halted near a waterfall for lunch, and after a brief rest continued their climb. An hour later Ranny, who was in the lead, drew up his mount and waited for the girls. With a sweep of his hand he indicated a fairly level stretch of land.

"Behold your property, Miss Drew!"

With a feeling akin to awe Nancy permitted her gaze to sweep over the vast expanse of territory.

"All that—mine?"

"Land is cheap this far north," Ranny smiled. "But it won't be so for long—not if gold should be found here."

"I feel like a feudal lord surveying his vast domain," Nancy smiled. "Father must have realized what an experience this would be when he sent me up here."

Slowly the group descended the knoll, and tied their horses to some trees near Pebble Creek.

"But where is the gold?" Bess queried in disappointment, as they walked about in the open stretches. "I haven't seen a single nug-get!"

Norman Ranny laughed heartily.

"Did you expect to find them kicking around underfoot?" he asked.

"Well, I didn't know where to look," Bess returned defensively.

"If you wish, we'll pan the creek," Ranny proposed. "I brought the necessary equipment."

"I want the first nugget," George cried gleefully.

The girls watched eagerly from the bank as the prospector panned for gold. At first it was exciting, but after a time the novelty of it wore off and they grew slightly tired of it.

"It doesn't look very promising," Bess commented wearily.

Just then Ranny took out a small object and tossed it over to Nancy.

"There's your nugget. It isn't worth much, but it's gold."

After that everyone wanted to try panning. The girls forgot all sense of time as they took turns using the man's equipment. Nancy found a similar lump of gold, while George, by diligent effort, acquired a slightly smaller one.

"I'm the only person that didn't get one," Bess grieved.

"Never mind. You may have the first one that was found," Nancy comforted.

While the girls had been engrossed at the stream, Ranny had wandered away to do a little prospecting on his own account. They came upon him working with his pick.

"Miss Drew, you may have something here

after all," he said quickly as Nancy paused beside him. "The gold in the creek doesn't amount to much, but it looks to me as if I have struck a vein! Should that be the case, your fortune will have been made!"

"I'll owe everything to you if I should strike gold!" Nancy assured Ranny gratefully. "I'm so ignorant about mining that I wouldn't know the difference between plain rock and gold ore."

"If you like, I'll do some real prospecting here when I have more time," the man said.

Before Nancy could thank him for his friendly offer, a monotonous drone was suddenly heard coming from above. She peered upward, to glimpse an airplane slowly circling over a large open stretch of land.

"Why, I believe it's going to come down," she cried.

Fearfully they all watched as the plane sideslipped earthward. A wing barely missed grazing the branch of a pine tree, which the pilot skillfully maneuvered to avoid.

The craft struck the narrow plot, and came bumping down over the rough ground. Before Nancy and her companions could reach the ship, two men leaped from the cockpit.

"What are you doing on private property?" one of them demanded of Ranny.

"This land belongs to me," Nancy maintained.

"Your claim is ridiculous," the other man snapped. "I am the owner of this ground. All of you must leave at once!"

Frightened, Bess and George backed away. Ranny and Nancy stood still.

"You are rank impostors!" the prospector shouted angrily. "I've seen other men of your stamp before."

He advanced menacingly, but Nancy placed a restraining hand upon his arm.

"Mr. Ranny, you may have made a mistake about this being my property," she said. "After all, the boundaries weren't surveyed."

"I've made no mistake," the man retorted, his lips drawn in a thin, hard line.

The two newcomers ignored the little party, and began to stake out a claim. They selected the hillside where Ranny had been digging.

"I might have known what you were after," the prospector said in a threatening voice. "You're nothing but low-down thieves!"

A fight would doubtless have resulted, had not another interruption come. An instant later another airplane loomed overhead. Everyone turned to look at it, as it slowly circled and presently landed beside the other ship. Several men sprang out and began to unload mining machinery and equipment from the cockpit.

"There's no use in opposing them," Nancy warned Ranny. "They intend to steal my property. We can't prevent them, for they greatly outnumber us."

She felt sick at heart as she realized how she had been tricked. Not for an instant did she doubt but that Tom Stripe and Raymond Niles were back of the scheme to steal her valuable mining land. She understood now why they had endeavored to reach the property before she did.

One of the men whom the others addressed as Buck Sawtice presently advanced toward the girls. His attitude was decidedly menacing.

"We can't have you hanging around here," he said curtly. "You'll have to get off this claim. It belongs to the Yellow Dawn."

"Is that a company or a disease?" George asked sarcastically.

"It's a mining company, young lady. Now, if you don't want any trouble, get going!"

Nancy signaled her companions to offer no resistance. Taking their cue from her, they followed her across the field.

However, the daughter of Carson Drew had no intention of abandoning the battle. She realized that it would be useless for her to enter into physical combat; if she wanted to defend her right, she would have to go to court.

"I must prove indisputably my claim to the land," she reflected, thinking rapidly. "But I must also be quick about it, or it will be too late to save the gold."

From the moment that Nancy had sighted the two airplanes, a daring plan had occurred to her. Glancing quickly over her shoulder to make sure that Sawtice and his companions did not see her, she crossed over to the nearest ship and addressed the pilot.

"Did Mr. Sawtice hire you to bring him here?"

"Yes, he did," the aviator returned crossly. "But he misrepresented the landing place and beat me down on the price."

"Are you under contract to wait for him?"

"No. But of course I expected he'd want me to take him back. Why did you want to know?"

"Because I must get to Wellington Lake as soon as possible," Nancy replied. "These men are crooks and are trying to cheat me out of my property. I must get to the nearest telegraph station and wire my father. Will you take me and my chums?"

The pilot debated but an instant.

"Jump in, and we'll be off," he cried, opening the door of the cabin.

Nancy turned to bid Norman Ranny goodbye. To her surprise, he announced that he intended to accompany her.

"I've decided to go to Windham, Miss Drew. I've been thinking about it all day. Even if Annette has changed in her feelings toward me, I can't bear to leave her alone in a hospital."

"I'm glad you've altered your original decision," Nancy said to him, her eyes shining.

Then she and her companions found seats in the cabin of the plane. The pilot soon had the propeller turning.

It was not until the roar and crack of the motor had rent the air that the men who had taken possession of the land realized what was happening. With a shout of anger they ran toward the aircraft. The pilot turned his ship in a narrow space. Then, taxiing to the far end of the open stretch, he came roaring down the field.

Buck Sawtice and his fellow conspirators were hopelessly outdistanced. However, the pilot was so intent upon avoiding them that he failed to observe another man who had darted from the bushes, and was now running directly into the path of the oncoming plane.

"Stop! Stop!" he shouted, waving his arms.

Nancy nearly fainted at thought of the impending tragedy.

CHAPTER XVII

A REUNION

"It's TOM STRIPE!" cried Nancy. "He'll be killed!"

The pilot swerved the plane barely in time to avoid disaster. It lifted from the ground, and rose sharply so as to miss by a fraction of an inch the pine trees that fringed the field.

"Whew!" Ranny ejaculated. "What a narrow escape!"

"Narrow for us, and narrow for Tom Stripe," Nancy declared, peering down at that scheming fellow on the ground from the cabin window. "I suspected he was party to a move to steal my land, and now I have definite proof of it."

"Do you suppose he's connected with the Yellow Dawn Mining Company?" George inquired thoughtfully.

"The company is in very poor repute up here in Canada," Ranny said. "It buys worthless land, issues stock upon it, and sells the valueless shares to innocent buyers in the United States."

"I'd expect Tom Stripe to be involved in a scheme like that," Nancy returned.

She was eager to get to a telegraph office with the least possible delay, for she intended to wire her father in River Heights and tell him exactly what had happened. She felt certain that by getting in touch with the Velvet Company he would be able to establish her claim to the property.

Nancy thought with a tug at her heart-strings of the old hollow oak near the Pierre Chap cabin. She had expected Norman Ranny to take her there the following day. Now that would be impossible.

"But I'll come back here inside of a week," she made up her mind. "Then I'll have a look at that famous old tree. Who knows? Perhaps I'll learn its secret!"

At Wellington Lake the party paused long enough for Nancy to communicate with Mrs. Donnelly and dispatch a wire to her father.

"I'll send word to Annette," Ranny decided, "and will tell her that as soon as I can possibly reach Windham I'll be at her bedside."

"Wire her by all means," Nancy urged, "Otherwise your sudden appearance might be too much of a shock for her to bear."

"I can't get to her quickly enough. If she in the meantime should take a turn for the worse, I should never forgive myself for having hesitated."

"We'll all go there in the plane," Nancy offered. "Be ready in half an hour."

While the girls were busily occupied at Mrs. Donnelly's boarding house, Ranny slipped away to a barber shop. At the appointed time he stood waiting for them at the landing field, but at first glance they failed to recognize him.

"Why, you've shaved off your beard," Bess gasped.

"You look years younger," George added admiringly.

During the plane ride from Wellington Lake to Windham, the girls could not refrain from stealing sly glances at Norman. They had never suspected that he was so striking in appearance. Unaware that he was the object of so much admiration, Ranny scarcely spoke during the flight, but sat gazing moodily out of the window.

The craft soon landed at a small commercial field near Windham, and the party continued to the Good Hope Hospital by automobile. The prospector grew increasingly nervous as they came within view of the institution.

"If anything has happened to Annette," he murmured, "I'll not be able to bear it."

Good news awaited the party on their arrival, however. Upon inquiry at the hospital, Nancy was informed that the authoress had been improving steadily ever since her operation.

"May I see her?" Ranny inquired eagerly.

The wire dispatched from Wellington Lake

had prepared the novelist for the visit of her former sweetheart. Her first feeling of excitement had subsided somewhat, but she was flushed and eager when he entered the room.

"Norman!" she exclaimed joyfully.

"Annette!" her lover cried, crossing toward her. "Can you ever forgive me?"

Nancy and her chums, who had waited in the corridor, were convinced that the reunion was to be a happy one. A few minutes later Annette and Norman insisted that the girls enter.

"I owe everything to you," the writer declared gratefully to Nancy. "As long as I live I'll never be able to thank you enough."

Everyone chatted excitedly for a few minutes, when a nurse presently came to warn the visitors that they must not stay too long. When out in the corridor again Ranny said soberly to Nancy:

"Annette and I know now that our separation was the result of an unfortunate circumstance. In some mysterious way the note she left for me in the hollow oak was exchanged for another. I'd give anything to learn who played that cruel trick on us."

"Perhaps we'll find out yet," Nancy told him.

Returning to the downstairs lobby, an attendant handed the girl a telegram which had just been delivered.

"I'm sure it's from Father," Nancy ex-

plained, tearing open the envelope. "I asked
him to wire me in care of the hospital."

She read the lengthy message, the expression
on her face denoting that its contents pleased
her.

"Father's coming here by plane," she announced. "He's as furious as I am about this
scheme to steal my land."

"And he's making a special trip here to help
you?" Bess asked.

"Not entirely. He also intends to look up
some data on the Taylor lawsuit case while
he's up North, so the trip will therefore serve
two purposes."

One of Norman Ranny's first missions during his stay in Windham was to visit his parents. Nancy and her chums agreed that after
picking up Mr. Drew at the airfield they should
join the prospector at his homestead.

The young people did not have long to wait,
however, for the attorney had chartered a plane
very shortly after his wire had been dispatched.
Nancy ran over to greet him when he stepped
from the cabin.

"Oh, Father, I'm so glad you're here," she
cried. "I think it will require all your legal
skill to save my property for me."

"That's quite likely," Mr. Drew returned
soberly. "Since I wired you I've acquired
some additional information."

"You mean bad news?"

"I'm afraid so, Nancy. Look at this message I received just as I took off from River Heights."

He produced a telegram from the Velvet Company for her to read.

"Cannot understand your communication," it said. "Nancy Drew assigned all rights in radio contest property to Yellow Dawn Mining Company for small consideration."

Nancy's eyes flashed angrily as she returned the missive to her father.

"It's an outrage! I have never assigned my rights to any company."

"You haven't signed your name to any papers?" Carson Drew inquired anxiously.

"I've signed nothing."

"Then either your signature has been forged, or else the Velvet Company is involved in this scheme to defraud you of your property."

"I have never heard of such high-handed robbery!"

"They haven't stolen the land yet," the lawyer told her grimly. "I know we're up against a clever group of schemers, but I think we shall be able to find a way to outwit them."

"I met one of the ringleaders," Nancy said. "I heard him called Buck Sawtice."

Carson Drew nodded.

"He is the president of the so-called Yellow Dawn Company. In reality he is the entire company, for the rest of the men do his bidding. Tom Stripe is one of his accomplices."

"I knew that, because he followed me to Wellington Lake and tried to prevent me from returning here."

Carson Drew's face darkened.

"I was afraid he might make trouble for you. That was one reason why I dropped everything and flew here to meet you."

"I'm glad you came," Nancy declared, putting her arms about him, "though I doubt even Tom Stripe would dare to attempt any violence."

"One can't be too sure, Nancy."

During the ride to the Ranny farmhouse Mr. Drew listened to his daughter's account of everything that had taken place in Canada. When they heard the automobile drive up the lane, Mr. and Mrs. Ranny rushed out to greet Nancy and shower their thanks upon her for bringing their son back home again.

"We were so worried after you took his picture with you," Mrs. Ranny said, smiling. "We realize now how foolish we were. Norman has told us of your wonderful kindness to him."

Nancy and her friends were escorted into the house. After the first pleasantries had been exchanged, the conversation turned to more serious subjects, in which Carson Drew chanced to mention Buck Sawtice of the Yellow Dawn Mining Company.

A strange expression came into Mrs. Ranny's eyes.

"Buck Sawtice!" she repeated.

"Yes. Do you know of him?" the attorney probed.

"He cost us our entire life savings," Mr. Ranny said gruffly. "He and another man talked us into buying some worthless mining stock."

"We lost everything," his wife added. "We were forced to leave our Canadian home and come here. Now we work from morning until night, barely making enough to live on."

"I wish I had known about it," Norman said contritely. "I would have shared anything in my possession with you."

"It wasn't your fault," his mother smiled fondly. "We couldn't tell you about our troubles, for we didn't know how to get in touch with you."

Carson Drew asked if he might see one of the shares of mining stock, and the owner obligingly found a certificate for him.

"May I keep it for a few days?" the attorney requested. "It should be of help to me in my case against these men."

"Keep it as long as you like," the farmer said. "It is of no use to us. I can't understand why we have saved it all these years."

A few minutes later Nancy and her friends took their departure. Norman Ranny accompanied his newly-made friends to the waiting automobile and addressed the Drew girl.

"Will you be returning to Canada?" he asked.

"I'm not certain yet, though I believe that is the plan. Are you going back with us?"

"That's what I wanted to talk to you about. As soon as Annette can be moved from the hospital, she is to be brought here."

"Oh, I'm so glad!" Nancy interrupted. "I know she'll improve rapidly under your mother's care."

"I feel sure she will, but she is worrying about something else. She told me today she is greatly worried about Grandfather Pierre. I promised her I would return to Canada and search for him."

"Then of course you'll go back with us."

Carson Drew, who had overheard the conversation, now walked over to where they were standing.

"I think everyone is eager to reach Wellington Lake with the least possible delay. I believe we should fly there tonight. There's no time to lose."

CHAPTER XVIII

THE SEARCH

CARSON DREW's plan was to institute legal proceedings against the Yellow Dawn Mining Company. During the plane ride to Wellington Lake that night he confided to Nancy that he suspected Tom Stripe and Buck Sawtice of being indirectly involved in the Marcus Taylor lumber case. He intended investigating the matter thoroughly before returning to River Heights.

"I never dreamed I'd get into so much trouble because I won the radio contest," Nancy remarked. "I thought the Velvet Company was an honest concern."

"I think it is. Naturally, the executives know nothing about you, so when they received the forged paper, which was doubtless the work of the Yellow Dawn officials, they more than likely never once doubted its authenticity."

"That mistake may cost me my land. I shouldn't feel so bad about it if it were an ordinary piece of property, but now that it seems as if gold may be found there I can't bear the thought of losing it."

"We'll fight for your rights to the bitter

end," the attorney assured her. "I feel partly responsible for all the trouble. Had I recorded your deed immediately after you received it, your position would have been far more secure."

"It certainly wasn't your fault, Father. We knew nothing about the ground. Had it turned out to be worthless I should doubtless have refused to accept it from the Velvet Company."

"We are up against a clever, unscrupulous group of men, and it will require all our ingenuity to combat them," concluded Carson Drew soberly.

Some minutes later the plane made a skillful landing at Wellington Lake, not far from Mrs. Donnelly's boarding house. Although the hour was late, a light still gleamed in the windows.

"She'll be surprised to see us return so soon," Nancy chuckled.

The woman was locking up for the night when the little party arrived. Learning that Nancy's party had left Windham without having had their evening meal, she insisted upon preparing a light repast for them before they should retire. Over their cups of cocoa, Mrs. Donnelly listened to Nancy's account of the plot to deprive her of the property.

"The Yellow Dawn Mining Company!" the woman exclaimed, upon hearing the name.

"Yes. Have you ever heard of it?" Nancy queried eagerly.

"Under most unpleasant circumstances. I once bought some mining stock from that concern. I should have known better, for I'm not easily taken in on business deals."

"Was the stock sold to you by a man named Buck Sawtice?" Mr. Drew queried.

"No! I'd never buy anything from that fellow!"

"What can you tell me about him?" the attorney asked quickly.

"I know him only by reputation, Mr. Drew. However, he is a partner in a lumber company which I suspect of being dishonest."

"I was hoping that I might uncover just such information," the lawyer returned, highly pleased. "I must run down the clue you have furnished me."

"I'm sorry I can't tell you any of the details," Mrs. Donnelly said regretfully, "though I can refer you to a man who might give you invaluable aid."

She wrote out the name of a local attorney and gave the paper to Carson Drew, who promised himself to call upon his contemporary at his earliest convenience.

It was after midnight when the consultation ended. The lights were then turned out, and everyone went to bed. At seven o'clock the following morning Nancy came downstairs to find that her father had arisen before she had.

"Mr. Drew went down to the village," Mrs.

Donnelly told her, "but said he expected to be back here in time for breakfast."

However, when an hour and a half had elapsed and still the attorney had not returned, Nancy grew troubled.

"If he doesn't get here soon it will ruin all our plans for the day," she declared.

At that moment Carson Drew was sighted coming up the path, walking briskly. His face wore an animated expression.

"Good news, Father?" Nancy asked.

"Yes. I have definite evidence that Sawtice is tied up in a scheme to rob Marcus Taylor of his lumber interests here in the North," he told her, sitting down to a hearty breakfast which Mrs. Donnelly had kept warm for him. "I think I've gathered enough material this morning to win the case."

"I'm glad of that," Nancy said. "If we could only recover my mining property everything ought to turn out splendidly."

"I'll visit your land today, if I can arrange it, and have a talk with Sawtice if he is working there," Carson Drew announced.

Norman Ranny, who was sitting near-by, overheard the remark.

"The matter can be easily arranged, Mr. Drew. I know this country as well as any guide you might engage. I have a boat here at Wellington Lake, and will be only too glad to take you with me."

"It doesn't seem fair to put you to so much trouble. If you will accept payment——"

"I couldn't, Mr. Drew. Your daughter has done me a service I shall never be able to re-pay her. Besides, I am eager to return to Mr. Chap's cabin on my own account."

"Then we'll accept your offer gratefully, Mr. Ranny. How soon can we start?"

"In fifteen minutes, if you like."

"I'll be ready," Mr. Drew promised.

"And so will we," Nancy added, speaking for her chums.

Carson Drew looked slightly troubled.

"Nancy, I don't like to disappoint you, but——"

"Father!"

"One can't be sure how this little adventure will end, my dear. Buck Sawtice is a tough customer, and may make plenty of trouble."

"All the more reason why we should be along!"

Mr. Drew smiled.

"I can't imagine what the Marvins and Faynes would do to me if any harm should be-fall their daughters."

"We've already met Buck Sawtice, and have escaped unscathed," George reminded him with a grin. "I vote that you take us all along."

With three against him, the attorney decided to give in.

"All right. But mind, if there's any trouble you three young ladies can expect to be sent straight back to Mrs. Donnelly's."

Nancy and her chums hurried to their rooms to don more suitable clothing than those they had on. By the time Norman Ranny had the boat and camping equipment ready the group was waiting for him at the pier.

The prospector chose a route similar to the one Pete Atkins had previously taken. The party rowed across Wellington Lake, made the portage, and then struck out again along the shore of Stewart Lake. Mr. Drew and Norman Ranny took turns at rowing. Since time was precious, a lunch Mrs. Donnelly had packed was eaten en route.

"We've made good time," the prospector declared after a time, squinting up at the sun. "That's the Chap cabin over yonder."

Far across the lake the girls caught a glimpse of the log structure. Nancy was quick to observe that no smoke was curling from the chimney.

"I hope we find Mr. Chap this time," she said, looking troubled. "You don't suppose he has met with an accident, do you?"

"He's probably somewhere in the vicinity," Mr. Drew returned.

"It isn't like Mr. Chap to be away for days at a time," Norman Ranny commented. "I'm beginning to feel worried about him."

With the goal so near, the prospector bent to his oars with a will. Ten minutes later the boat grated upon the sandy beach.

While the guide and Mr. Drew dragged the craft from the water, Nancy, George and Bess ran on ahead to find out if Mr. Chap were at home. As the former emerged into the clearing, she halted abruptly. The cabin had been boarded up!

"Well, of all things!" she exclaimed in astonishment. "What in the world does this mean?"

Bess and George were equally bewildered. They ran back to the beach to tell the men the disappointing news, and the two at once came to view the building for themselves.

"I can't understand it," the prospector said, gloomily examining the covered windows and door. "It looks as if Grandfather Chap may have returned here yesterday and closed up the place himself. As far as I know, he expected to remain here for the summer."

"His crops are planted," Nancy observed. "And the cupboards inside the house are filled with perishable groceries."

"I don't like the appearance of things," Ranny confessed.

"Do you think he has met with foul play?" Nancy asked quickly.

"I don't know what to think. Tom Stripe and Raymond Niles acted suspicious, to say the least. They tied me up and left me alone to die. If Grandfather Chap happened to have been in their way, they doubtless would have treated him the same way."

"Would it be possible to break into the house and make certain that he isn't a prisoner inside?" Nancy asked.

"I think I can pry off one of the boards over the rear window," Ranny decided, making an inspection.

After considerable trouble the prospector succeeded in removing the barrier. While Nancy and her companions waited outside, he climbed through the window and disappeared within. Shortly thereafter he returned.

"Everything is just exactly as we left it," he reported. "Mr. Chap isn't here."

He carefully boarded up the window again.

"I suppose there's nothing to do but to continue on our journey," Nancy said in disappointment. "It begins to look as if the elderly man really has left the place for good."

Gloomily the party returned to the beach. While Nancy and her chums took care of the oars and light equipment, Carson Drew and Norman Ranny carried the boat a short distance to the rushing stream, which offered rapid transportation deeper into the woods. After an uneventful and somewhat silent journey the craft was finally drawn up near the Dawson cabin.

"How is Pete?" Nancy questioned anxiously, after she had greeted its mistress.

"Greatly improved," the woman assured her. "This morning he ate a hearty meal and walked about for a few minutes. Of course, he's still very weak."

"That's only natural after his receiving such a hard blow," Nancy smiled. "Where is he now? I should like to have him meet my father."

"He and Jake went out to the barn a few minutes ago. I'll call them."

There was no need for her to do so, however. As she went over to the door Mrs. Dawson saw her older son hurrying toward the house.

"I tried to stop him but I couldn't!" he exclaimed, when he was within earshot. "There's no telling what he may do!"

"Jake, what are you talking about?" his mother demanded.

"Pete Atkins!" the boy explained. "He said he's going to run down Tom Stripe and square things up!"

CHAPTER XIX

Mr. Drew's Strategy

It was too late to overtake the guide. Bent upon redressing the wrong which had been done him by Tom Stripe, Pete Atkins had slipped away into the dense woods, all the while avoiding the well-worn trails.

"What a pity he didn't wait," Mr. Drew said regretfully. "Soon the authorities will be here."

This was news to the others, since the attorney had neglected to mention the fact that he had called upon the sheriff that morning while in Wellington Lake. There he had received the assurance that men would be sent immediately to protect Nancy's property.

"An expert surveyor will come along, too," Mr. Drew told his daughter. "After he has gone over the land we'll know exactly where we stand. Until we are absolutely certain that the property is the same as that deeded to you by the Velvet Company, we shall have to move slowly."

"How many men will the sheriff bring along with him?" Norman Ranny inquired.

"Not very many, I am afraid. It would be a

good idea if we could round up some others. Buck Sawtice and his men are likely to offer us armed resistance.''

''I think we could find a number of woodsmen who might be willing to join the posse,'' the prospector said slowly.

''I'll be glad to go,'' Mr. Dawson spoke up. ''And both of my sons are mighty handy when it comes to protectin' property.''

''We hope there will be no necessity for a fight,'' Mr. Drew returned, ''though we shall have to be prepared for it.''

Norman Ranny knew of several families living in the immediate vicinity. While he rode in one direction to spread word of the gathering posse, Nancy and George with young Jake went the opposite way to ask for similar help. They returned to the Dawson cabin with several neighbors riding behind them.

''I feel like a modern Joan of Arc leading her warriors to battle,'' Nancy confessed with a smile to George as they dismounted. ''I shouldn't want to miss this adventure for anything in the world.''

The girls discovered that during their absence the Wellington Lake sheriff and his deputies had arrived. The yard swarmed with horsemen. A few minutes later Norman Ranny returned with additional numbers.

As the group waited for orders to start off, Mr. Drew crossed over to the place where the girls were standing with Mrs. Dawson. Nancy surmised what his purpose was at once.

"Now, Father, don't tell us we can't go," she forestalled him. "With all these men along to protect us, you surely can't say it won't be safe."

"That's just what I did intend to say, you young tease!"

"We'll be very careful, if you'll only permit us to go along."

"The trip will be a hazardous one at best, Nancy. I'll not be able to keep an eye on all of you. If there only could be some way whereby we might keep in close communication with one another, even though separated——"

"I know of a way!" Nancy cried, her eyes lighting up with inspiration.

"How?" Mr. Drew smiled.

"Why, the old hollow oak tree!"

"I don't understand."

"You couldn't, because I've never told you about it. It happens that on the Chap property there stands an old hollow oak tree which would be an ideal place in which to leave a message. I propose that should any one of us get into trouble, that person will endeavor to drop a note in this famous tree."

It was obvious, however, that Carson Drew was not particularly impressed with the idea.

"I've never even seen this tree," he protested.

"We can have Mr. Ranny point it out so that everyone will be certain of its location," Nancy went on, growing more enthusiastic as she spoke. "He told me only a few minutes ago that we would pass close to it on our way to visit my property."

Mr. Drew conceded defeat.

"If I turn this idea down, I feel sure you'll think up another," he laughed. "I still am convinced that it is unwise to take you with me, though I suppose I must give in."

"How can we leave any notes when we have neither paper nor pencil?" Bess questioned doubtfully.

Nancy ran to the house for the necessary articles, which she distributed among her friends.

"I know you think the plan won't work," she told her father a little later as he assisted her into the saddle, "but you never can tell."

"Perhaps it isn't as wild a scheme as I thought at first, Nancy. At least I'll reserve judgment until after I've seen this mysterious old oak."

The posse set off through the timber, and slowly began the steep, rocky ascent. Nancy, her father and her chums were mounted on spirited horses. Gradually they forged ahead until they eventually found themselves leading the cavalcade. Then presently the Drew girl moved ahead of the party eagerly. As she rounded a bend in the trail, she suddenly halted her horse, for through the trees she had caught a glimpse of a dark object lying prone upon the ground. She was almost certain it was a man. Her first thought had been that Buck Sawtice and some of his confederates were watching the trail.

"I must be careful not to lead the party into a trap," she reasoned to herself.

Waiting motionless, she watched the figure in the bushes. It did not move.

"What do you see?" called her father.

Convinced that her fears were groundless, Nancy sprang from the saddle before answering. Tossing the reins over a small bush, she pushed aside the foliage. There she came upon Pete Atkins, who was lying face downward on the ground.

"Pete!" she cried fearfully.

The guide made no response as the girl attempted to turn him over. Then she noticed that his shirt was saturated with blood. Alarmed, Nancy ran back, calling for help.

"Come quickly, Father!" she cried. "Pete Atkins has been wounded!"

All the riders urged their horses on to a faster pace. Upon reaching the bend in the trail, they hastily dismounted.

"Careful, men," the sheriff warned them. "This may be a trick."

On the alert for any trouble, the men followed Nancy to the place where Pete Atkins lay.

"Pete's been shot. Comb the woods and see if you can find the person who did it!" the sheriff ordered, bending down to examine the guide.

He had brought along a first-aid kit, and after probing about for the bullet, bandaged the wounded shoulder. As the officer worked, the guide opened his eyes and groaned with pain.

"Who did it, Pete?" the sheriff asked gently.

The man was too exhausted to answer him.

"It must have been an unprovoked attack," Norman Ranny announced furiously. "I imagine Pete was shot from behind!"

The members of the posse were returning from their unsuccessful search of the surrounding woods. Not a living soul had been sighted.

"Will Pete live?" Nancy asked the sheriff anxiously, as they got out of hearing of the wounded man.

"Yes, I think his chances are very good," she was told. "But he's so weak from loss of blood that we won't be able to take him with us."

"Why can't you assign one of the men to remain with him?"

"That's probably the best thing to do," the sheriff agreed.

One of the men from Wellington Lake was

selected for that duty. After Pete had been carefully moved to a more comfortable place and laid upon an improvised bed of blankets, the party prepared to proceed onward again.

It was apparent to everyone that an entirely new feeling had come over the men. At first they had regarded the expedition as more or less of an adventure. Now, infuriated at the heartless treatment Pete had received, they were eager to avenge themselves upon his assailant. Their faces were grim and determined.

"I don't like the looks of things," Carson Drew said anxiously as he assisted Nancy to mount. "I fear that this shooting forebodes trouble. I only wish that you and your chums were back safe with Mrs. Dawson."

"We'll be careful," Nancy promised. "Please don't worry about us."

"I can't help it, for all the responsibility rests on me. However, I've been thinking over that idea of yours, and if it will work, maybe you'll be all right."

"You mean the one about the oak tree?"

"Yes. If anything should go wrong and we were to become separated, try to drop a message in the hollow trunk."

"I most certainly will. But I doubt if anything serious is going to happen. We have so many guards to protect us."

"I hope you're right, Nancy."

As they continued along the trail at a much swifter pace than before, the attorney rode close to the girls. At length the posse arrived at the knoll from which Nancy had previously viewed her property. Here the riders halted for orders.

Nancy, her father, and Norman Ranny all dismounted in order that the girl might obtain a more advantageous position from which to view the scene in the valley below. Several men were working feverishly near the cliff where Ranny had discovered gold.

"There's Buck Sawtice directing the removal of the ore," the prospector announced bitterly, training his powerful field glass upon one of the men.

He handed it over to Nancy.

"I take it that Sawtice will refuse to allow our man to survey the property," Carson Drew remarked, thinking aloud.

"That's to be expected," the prospector agreed. "He'll not give up the land if he can help it."

"No. But if we take the camp by surprise, the chance of their resisting will be much less."

"We can descend from the knoll without being seen from below," Ranny stated. "The tall bushes make a perfect screen."

So saying, he indicated a trail Nancy had not seen during her previous visit. The two men returned to the sheriff to give their orders.

Nancy was about to follow, when a slight sound in the bushes attracted her attention. She saw a man crawling rapidly on his hands and knees through the foliage and then scramble to his feet, to race madly toward the camp below.

"A lookout!" Nancy called in frantic warning. "Stop him before he gives an alarm!"

CHAPTER XX

STARTLING INFORMATION

It was too late now to overtake the lookout, for he had dashed far down the steep slope. Carson Drew ordered his followers to descend upon the camp at a gallop, for he saw there was no further advantage to be gained by cautious maneuvers.

Nancy sprang into the saddle. With her chums riding beside her, she trailed the posse into the valley. Once George's horse stumbled in the loose earth, but the girl clung tightly to her mount, so was not thrown.

Buck Sawtice had been warned of the approach, but readily saw that since his men were outnumbered, it would be useless to offer any resistance. He therefore changed to more strategic tactics, and came forward to greet Carson Drew with a show of civility. The attorney adopted a similar conciliatory attitude.

"There's been a good deal of misunderstanding about this property," Mr. Drew began. "According to a deed which my daughter holds, this land belongs to her."

Sawtice tried to look surprised.

"It cannot belong to your daughter, for I hold the title to it. I have received a deed from the Velvet Company."

"Have you the paper with you?" Carson Drew queried.

"Well, no, I haven't."

"Then I'm sure you'll have no objection to our surveyor staking out my daughter's plot. Before we make any claim to this property we must be absolutely certain we are right."

Buck Sawtice obviously objected to such a proposal, and seemed to be on the verge of angrily refusing the request, when his eyes wandered to the grim line of armed men who stood directly behind the attorney. Then he changed his mind again.

"I should be very glad to have you survey the land," he said coldly. "I feel sure that it will aid in proving my right to the property."

While the surveyor and his helpers were setting up their equipment, Nancy wandered aimlessly about the tract of land. She was somewhat disturbed to note that Sawtice and his men had begun to blast in the cliff where Ranny had discovered gold.

She bent down to examine an oddly-colored piece of rock. Convinced that it contained streaks of the precious yellow metal, she slipped it into her pocket, intending to ask Mr. Ranny's opinion about it later.

Suddenly there came to her ears the sound of

a conversation being carried on in low tones. The speakers were screened from view by bushes and rocks, but Nancy crept closer, suspecting that they might perhaps be Sawtice's men. Even at such a range the conversation was unintelligible.

Suddenly it dawned upon her that the two men were speaking in French. She had diligently studied the language in school, but this conversation moved so rapidly that it was difficult for her to catch all that was being said.

"I can jot down the words now and translate them later," she told herself, drawing a pencil and pad from her pocket. "It will be much easier when I see them written out."

She succeeded in catching several phrases, which appeared formidable to her as she wrote them on paper. Fearful lest she miss something of even greater importance, she strained to hear everything that was being said.

Suddenly somebody tapped her on the shoulder. Nancy stifled a scream as she wheeled about to face Tom Stripe.

"You! Here!" she gasped.

The man was glancing at the notebook, trying to make out what she had written.

"Don't look so startled," he smirked. "What are you writing, anyway?"

Relieved, Nancy realized that the man could not read French.

"I always carry a notebook with me when

I go any place," she evaded neatly. "I like to jot down my impressions of the scenery and the various people."

This answer seemed to appease Stripe. However, his tone became slightly menacing as he said, "This isn't a very healthy place for you to be taking notes."

"It's my land, Tom Stripe!"

"It *was* your land, you mean," he sneered. "I gave you a chance to sell and you wouldn't take it. Now it's too late."

"That remains to be seen. If I should lose the property, I'd always be glad that I refused to have business dealings with a man like you!"

Tom Stripe moved closer, and for an instant Nancy thought he was going to strike her. But her significant glance in the direction of the surveyor, who was working not far away, warned him that if he should molest her she would scream for help. With an angry gesture the fellow turned and then walked away.

Nancy raced back to see if she could find her father or Mr. Ranny, but they were nowhere to be seen. Bess and George, who were sitting on a boulder watching the surveyor, greeted their chum eagerly.

"Where have you been, Nancy?" Bess asked. "We were beginning to grow alarmed, for George thought she saw Tom Stripe skulking around here."

"You are quite right," Nancy returned, addressing the other girl. "I met him just a minute ago."

"Did he try to harm you?" George queried anxiously.

"I think he would have liked to, but he lacked the necessary courage with so many persons near by. It certainly was lucky for me that he never learned French."

"What are you talking about, Nancy?" Bess asked in bewilderment.

For answer, her chum laughingly withdrew the notebook from her pocket. Her face grew unusually serious as she read what she had copied. After she had explained the significance of the writing, she translated the message for them.

"'Old recluse has been sent by new owner here on wild chase. Meanwhile, men are robbing fellow of his property—say he will never come back alive.'"

"How dreadful!" Bess exclaimed, as she peered over Nancy's shoulder to re-read the message herself.

"I'm not surprised that it almost frightened you to death when Tom Stripe tried to translate your notes," George added. "Oh, do you suppose Mr. Chap really has been harmed?"

"He has been tricked, and his life is in danger. The men said a great deal more, but they talked so rapidly I couldn't catch everything."

"What can we do to save poor Mr. Chap?" Bess asked, greatly worried.

"I'm going to tell Mr. Ranny and Father," Nancy declared. "They may decide to organize a searching party."

George glared at Buck Sawtice, who was working a short distance away.

"I'll venture *he* could tell where Mr. Chap has gone," she said furiously. "For half a cent I'd walk over there and accuse him."

She arose from the rock with the idea of carrying out this intention, when Nancy caught her by the arm.

"Don't do anything rash, George. We mustn't let anyone suspect what we know. If we do, we will lose all chance of finding Mr. Chap."

"I suppose you're right, Nancy. I know I am inclined to be too hot-headed."

"There's Mr. Ranny now," Bess indicated.

"I'll go over and talk to him," Nancy said hastily.

She drew the prospector aside and showed him the notebook. His face grew stern as he read the words written in French.

"Tom Stripe and Buck Sawtice are back of all this!" he cried angrily. "I'll have it out with them right away and learn the truth of the matter."

"That's what George wanted to do," Nancy smiled. "But I believe that's not the best way. We haven't enough evidence to accuse anyone as yet. I thought that if you would scout around a little and follow Stripe and his friends, we might perhaps find Mr. Chap and at the same time get proof of his abduction."

At these words Norman Ranny smothered his anger, for he realized that Nancy's suggestion was a wise one. After he had warned the girl to destroy her notes lest they fall into the hands of someone who might be able to read them, he moved swiftly away.

Nancy did not have an opportunity until some time later to tell her father what she had overheard. When he joined her after a lengthy talk with the surveyor, he, too, had news to report.

"I'm making excellent progress in accumulating data to be used in the Taylor lumber case," Carson Drew declared enthusiastically. "The surveyor gave me a few tips which I mean to investigate as soon as I return to Wellington Lake."

"I'm glad of that," his daughter replied. "Two purposes will be accomplished by the trip."

"Of course we can't do much here until after the survey has been made."

"I realize that, Dad; in fact, I've not given much thought to my property rights since we arrived here. I've been too worried about poor Mr. Chap."

"No doubt he's just away on a vacation somewhere, Nancy."

"That's what I thought when we saw his cabin all boarded up, but I know such is not the case. I have evidence that Sawtice spirited Pierre Chap from his home for the purpose of stealing his property."

She produced her notes. After Mr. Drew had carefully read them Nancy tore them into tiny bits which she scattered to the winds.

"What do you think about this, Father?" she queried.

"It looks as if you have uncovered a real clue, Nancy. Of course, what you overheard may have been mere, idle gossip with but a slight foundation of truth in it."

"I realize that, but even if the evidence should not bear weight in court, it serves as something upon which to work. I've asked Norman Ranny to do a little scouting before we openly accuse Sawtice."

"You've handled the matter very well," Mr. Drew praised. "If nothing should develop within the next few hours I shall organize searching parties and comb the woods for Mr. Chap."

In spite of her father's words, Nancy did not feel that she was doing much to help bring about the return of Pierre Chap. The longer she thought about it the more worried did she become. She feared that the delay of a few hours might mean the difference between life and death.

She glanced anxiously about the camp for Norman Ranny, but the prospector had disappeared. Thinking that he might still be at the place where the horses had been tethered, the girl ran over to look. As luck would have it, the prospector was just then riding away.

"Mr. Ranny!" she called frantically.

The man heard her, and turned his horse about.

"Take me with you," Nancy pleaded.

"But it won't be safe for you where I'm going," he protested.

"Oh, but I've changed my mind about wanting you to look for Mr. Chap," she told him breathlessly. "Instead, I want you to take me to the hollow oak!"

"The hollow oak!"

Nancy was busy untying her horse.

"Yes. I've just had a 'hunch' regarding it. I think it may offer a very valuable clue as to what has become of Pierre Chap!"

CHAPTER XXI

THE HIDDEN CHEST

IF NORMAN RANNY had any doubts regarding
the advisability of the journey to the famous
old "letter box" oak, he kept them to himself.
So he and Nancy Drew rode over the narrow
trail in silence, until finally they came near
a waterfall.

"This is the northern edge of Pierre Chap's
land," the prospector explained. "It is one of
the most beautiful places in this section of the
country. Years ago Annette and I would often
meet here."

He led the way through a lane of stately
trees. As they approached a giant gnarled oak
which stood by itself in a tiny clearing, Norman Ranny paused. As he did so, an expression of mingled pain and joy came over his
face.

The tree was well over a hundred years old,
Nancy felt sure; never before had she beheld a
more magnificent specimen. The prospector
indicated a dead limb which had split from the
trunk.

"That is the bough that almost finished me.
I guess this old oak must have a sort of kindred

feeling for me; otherwise I shouldn't be here now."

Nancy crossed over to the ancient tree, gazing with renewed interest at its bigness.

"Mr. Ranny, please tell me where the hollow 'letter box' is," she eagerly said to her companion.

Ranny showed her a cleverly concealed cavity far up the trunk at a point where two of the boughs came together. It was nearly out of reach for one of Nancy's height, so she stood up on tiptoe to peer into it.

"It seems to extend far back into the tree."

"Yes," the prospector agreed. "At one time a swarm of bees decided to adopt that hollow, and until we could get rid of them Annette and I thought we'd lose our letter box."

Nancy thrust her hand into the opening, but brought it out empty.

"It looks as if my hunch weren't such a good one, Mr. Ranny."

"What did you expect to find?"

"I don't know," Nancy admitted. "Something just seemed to tell me to come to this old oak. I had a feeling that I might find a communication of some kind about Mr. Chap."

"That is quite unlikely."

"I suppose I have brought you here on a wild chance," Nancy said apologetically. "But now that we've made the trip, I guess I may as well examine the hollow carefully. Would you please lift me up, Mr. Ranny, so that I might run my hand far back into the cavity?"

Obligingly he raised her, and Nancy once more thrust her arm into the opening.

"I can feel something!" the girl announced excitedly. "It rustles just like paper!"

"Probably it's a dead leaf."

"No, it's a piece of paper," Nancy maintained. "But it's just beyond my reach."

"Let me go after it," the prospector urged, beginning to share in her enthusiasm.

Nancy made way for him, but the paper was too far down in the hollow for even his grasp.

"Wait. I'll get a stick," the girl cried.

She found one with a knob on the end. Ranny held her up again. This time she was successful in raking in the paper. Triumphantly she then held it up to the light.

"It's a message! It is!" she cried.

"Read it," Ranny commanded tensely.

It was difficult for Nancy to keep her voice steady as she began:

" 'Fearing for my life at the hands of Buck Sawtice and his gang, I am placing this message in the hollow oak, trusting that if anything should happen to me it will some day be found.

" 'I hope that the one who discovers this communication will be you, Annette, my granddaughter, who married the Ranny boy against my will. I realize now that my attitude was misguided, and I beg your forgiveness for having attempted to prevent your wedding.

" 'I have hidden my money at the base of this tree. The inheritance is yours, Annette. Keep it with my blessing, and try to forgive your loving grandfather, Pierre Chap.' "

"Let me read the message for myself!" Norman Ranny cried as Nancy finished. "I can't believe that I heard you correctly. Is it possible that Grandfather Pierre believed that Annette and I were married?"

"It appears that he did," Nancy returned, handing him the note for his inspection. "What does he mean by the reference to his money? Do you suppose he actually hid a treasure here beside the tree?"

"Grandfather Pierre never had a great deal of confidence in banks. He hoarded funds which he kept in the house."

"Then the treasure must be buried here, as he states. If we only had something with which to dig!"

"I'll go back and get a spade. It won't take long. You're not afraid to remain here alone, are you, Miss Drew?"

"No," Nancy said staunchly. "Only try to hurry as fast as you can, and be careful that no one follows you back here."

"I'll return in fifteen minutes if luck is with me," the prospector promised.

When she was left alone in the still, deep woods, Nancy began to wish that she had accompanied her friend. It made her a trifle nervous to feel that she was the sole guard over what might prove to be a fair-sized fortune. As she again moved over to the hollow oak, a slight sound in the bushes caused her to start. What she heard was only a wild animal, however.

Nancy occupied her time trying to determine the exact spot where the treasure might be buried, and soon located a patch of recently turned earth.

"This must be where the money is hidden," she said to herself. "Oh, I wish Mr. Ranny would hurry!"

She sat down, her back against the gnarled tree, and waited. Nervously she clasped and unclasped a gold bracelet she was wearing. Fifteen minutes passed. Then ten more. Still nothing to break the deep silence!

Suddenly there came the clatter of hoofs along the trail, and Nancy jumped up quickly. Not until Norman Ranny appeared did she relax her rigid attitude.

"Did I frighten you?" the prospector asked.

"A little," Nancy admitted. "I wasn't sure that it was you."

She thereupon indicated the patch of loose earth and he began to dig industriously. Presently his spade struck something hard.

"There's a cache here, all right!" he declared tensely.

Turning over a little more of the earth, the man uncovered a metal chest. Removing it from the ground, he handed it over for Nancy to open.

With trembling fingers the girl unfastened the clasp, and the lid fell back. Within the chest there lay stack upon stack of bills, as well as some loose ones and a number of gold coins.

As Nancy and Ranny peered down at the treasure, a trifle dazed by the discovery, a playful wind caught up a few of the bills and scattered them upon the grass. Nancy slammed down the lid of the chest, and the two darted about, picking up the scattered money.

"I guess we have it all," she said at length, returning the loose bills to the container.

"What shall we do with the chest?" Ranny asked with a worried frown. "We dare not take it back to camp."

"I suppose the safest thing will be to bury it again."

"But not in the same hole."

They looked about the clearing for a suitable hiding place. Nancy finally found one near a sandstone boulder. Ranny dug a new hole, and with a careful glance in all directions to make certain that no one was watching, the two deposited the chest in it.

"Don't forget to fill up the old hole," Nancy

cautioned, as she tramped down the loose dirt over the chest and scattered dry leaves to conceal their work.

The prospector carefully refilled the gap in the earth beneath the old oak, and smoothed down the surface dirt.

"There, that's the very best we can do," he announced, picking up his spade. "We may as well get away from here."

"The sooner the better," Nancy agreed.

They mounted their horses and rode rapidly in the direction of the camp. Both Nancy and her companion avoided speaking of Pierre Chap. The discovery of the note he had left in the hollow tree had chilled their hearts with the fear that the old man might be dead.

"Buck Sawtice holds the clue to his fate," Nancy thought. "If I only knew of some way in which to force that man to reveal the truth!"

They were now drawing near the mining camp. Nancy suddenly glanced down at her wrist, and noticed that her gold bracelet was missing. At her cry of alarm Ranny halted his pony to inquire what was wrong.

"I've lost my bracelet!"

"You must have dropped it on the trail."

"Either that, or else it fell from my wrist when I was sitting by the oak tree. I remember unclasping it. If anyone should find it near the place where the treasure is hidden, he might grow suspicious as to why we were there. It had my name inside."

"We'd better ride back for it."

"I don't so much mind losing the bracelet, even though it is a good one," Nancy said apologetically as they turned their horses, "but I am afraid it would reveal a clue to the finder, something I don't want known just now."

"Especially if it should come into the hands of one of Buck Sawtice's men," Ranny added. "They doubtless know Grandfather Pierre hid his money somewhere near here and are trying to force him to reveal the hiding place."

"I can't bear to think of anybody being tortured," Nancy shuddered.

Norman Ranny's lips drew into a hard line.

"I'd not put anything past Buck Sawtice and his gang," he said.

Within a few minutes they drew near the hollow oak and tied their horses in a clump of bushes some distance away. As they walked along the path, Nancy caught sight of the footprints of a man in the moist earth, footprints which did not in the least resemble Ranny's. She called her companion's attention to them.

"The print is a fresh one," he declared, stooping to examine it. "Someone has passed by this way since we left here a few minutes ago."

They proceeded at a more cautious pace. As they drew near the clearing they halted, and peered through the bushes.

Nancy started. She saw a man examining the soft earth near the base of the hollow oak. It was none other than Tom Stripe!

"He must have followed me from camp when I went for the spade," Ranny whispered.

"Do you think he saw us dig up the treasure?"

"I doubt it. He seems a little suspicious of the loose earth, but doesn't quite know what to make of it."

"I hope we gathered up all the bank-notes that blew away," Nancy whispered nervously. "If he were to find one of those he'd be almost certain to suspect the truth."

As she spoke, they heard Tom Stripe utter a low exclamation of surprise. He reached down and picked up an object from the loose dirt.

"He has found my bracelet!" Nancy gasped.

CHAPTER XXII

The Lost Bracelet

"He has found my bracelet!" Nancy repeated, as she recognized the object Tom Stripe had picked up from the soft earth.

The man did not seem to know what to make of the discovery, for he turned the trinket over and over in his hand, finally placing it in his pocket. Glancing carefully about him, he walked over to a clump of bushes not far from the place where Nancy and Norman Ranny were hiding, and drew forth a spade. As he walked back to the old oak he began to turn up the loose earth at its base.

Nancy watched him, fascinated. How had the man known that the treasure chest had been hidden beneath the oak? She was convinced that he had not guessed the truth, and that the bracelet had not furnished the clue. He had brought his spade to the site for the express purpose of looking for the buried money.

Tensely the two waited. Would Tom Stripe find the new hiding place after discovering the hole was empty? He was already a bit suspicious. They could hear him muttering under his breath as he rested upon the steel tool.

"This must be the place," Nancy caught the words. "It fits old Chap's description to a 'T.' Looks like someone has beat me here."

Convinced that Stripe had obtained inside information concerning the hidden chest, Nancy whispered a plan to her companion. Ranny nodded that he understood, and crept back to the place where the horses had been left. He returned a moment later, bringing with him a long coil of rope.

"Do you think you can lasso him from this distance?" Nancy whispered anxiously. "If you miss, he'll get away."

Ranny did not reply. Instead, he stepped out into the open, his rope swinging. It swished swiftly through the air, and settled neatly over Tom Stripe's shoulders.

Taken completely by surprise, the man dropped his spade and uttered a terrified yell. As he struggled to free himself, Ranny drew the rope taut about his captive's waist.

"Let me go!" the prisoner snarled.

"All in good time," Nancy replied pleasantly. "Tie him to the tree, Mr. Ranny."

Tom Stripe made a desperate effort to free himself, but was unable to move. The prospector then trussed him securely to the trunk of the old oak.

"What do you want?" the prisoner demanded fearfully. "If it's the money, I have never found it."

"So we noticed," Nancy responded. "You may as well tell us the truth, Tom Stripe, for it will go much easier with you if you do. Who told you about Mr. Chap's money?"

The prisoner maintained a sullen silence.

"What have you done with the recluse?" Nancy demanded sharply.

The only answer was a sardonic smile.

Ranny tried the next question. Though he threatened the man, he could not get a word from him. Realizing that such tactics were useless, Nancy and her guide retired a few paces away for a consultation.

"What shall we do?" the girl asked, almost at her wits' end. "We must make him talk, for I feel certain he can tell us where Grandfather Pierre is."

"I think I can make him tell the truth," Ranny returned grimly.

"We mustn't harm him in any way. I would never consent to that."

"I'll not hurt him, but I intend to give him a good scare. Whatever I do, back me up in it. Don't lose your nerve. I think he'll talk!"

Nancy was almost as troubled as was the prisoner when the prospector began to gather together a pile of dry sticks.

"What are you going to do?" Stripe demanded uneasily.

"Oh, just build a little fire. Still think you don't care to talk, eh?"

Stripe ignored the question, but Nancy observed that beads of perspiration had broken out over the man's face. She began to feel a bit sorry for him.

Ranny brought the pile of dry wood and placed it at the base of the oak tree.

"This is just an old trick the Indians sometimes used with their prisoners," he remarked pleasantly.

Tom Stripe's face became convulsed with terror. Yet even then he would not give in.

"You haven't the nerve to go through with it!" he taunted.

"Wait and see," Ranny countered.

After he had finished his somewhat elaborate preparations, he drew a match from his pocket. Stripe watched with fascinated eyes as the prospector lighted the dry wood. A tiny flame leaped up, licking at the prisoner's boots.

It was all Nancy could do to keep from pleading with Ranny to extinguish the blaze. Yet she recalled his promise that he would not harm the man.

"Now will you talk?" Ranny asked.

Tom Stripe moistened his lips. He gazed down at the fire. The last shred of his courage vanished.

"Put out the fire! Put it out!" he screamed. "I'll tell you the truth!"

Nancy darted forward to help Ranny stamp out the flames. The prisoner had not been hurt, though he was almost hysterical from fright.

"All right. Out with the story," the prospector ordered.

"I knew all about the hidden chest," Stripe gasped. "I tortured Pierre Chap and forced him to tell me where he had hidden it."

At this admission Ranny involuntarily stepped forward as if to strike the prisoner. However, Nancy placed a restraining hand upon his arm. With an effort he controlled his temper and listened to the remainder of the story.

"Where is Mr. Chap now?" Nancy questioned, after Stripe had finished relating the manner in which he had overpowered the old man.

The captive hesitated, then said:

"He's hidden in an old cave about six miles from here. It's called Gordon's Grotto."

"I know where you mean," Ranny nodded.

"You stay here and watch Stripe," Nancy suggested. "I'll race back to camp and tell the sheriff. The posse can start for Gordon's Grotto in a few minutes."

The prospector wrote out complete directions for reaching the cave. With the notation safe in her pocket, Nancy galloped back to the mining camp. As she dismounted at her destination, a man came to meet her. With an unpleasant start she recognized him as Raymond Niles.

"So you're here, too!"

"Oh, I've been close by all the while," the man smiled disarmingly. "But I've taken no part in this scheme to defraud you of your land."

"Oh, no!" Nancy retorted sarcastically.

"It's the truth. I did try to buy your property, but I have a great distaste for the whole affair now. Since I've met you and found you such a charming young lady——"

"I don't care for your admiration, Mr. Niles! Please permit me to pass."

With a toss of her head Nancy moved past him and went to find the sheriff. She quickly informed him of all that had occurred near the hollow oak.

"I'll send some of my deputies there without delay to take Stripe prisoner," the man promised. "I'll dispatch another group to Gordon's Grotto."

At Nancy's suggestion, great care was taken to prevent Buck Sawtice from suspecting what was going on. So engrossed was he at the moment in arguing with the surveyor, that he observed nothing else.

Not until the two groups of men rode away did he note that anything unusual was occurring. Then he strode angrily over to Carson Drew.

"What is it you're up to now?" he demanded.

"I'm sure I don't know what you mean," the attorney retorted.

"You know well enough! But I'm tired of all this trouble. I'm willing to make your daughter a fair offer for her land!"

Carson Drew could not restrain a smile. He had seen the man talking with the surveyor, and surmised that the latter had refused to be bribed or intimidated.

"What do you consider a fair price, Mr. Sawtice?"

"A thousand dollars."

"That's not very much for property that contains gold," Mr. Drew smiled.

"It's my best offer. If you don't take it I may not be so generous again." So saying, Sawtice turned and walked away.

Carson Drew sought his daughter to tell her the latest development. As they were discussing it the surveyor joined them.

"I've practically finished my work," he announced.

"And is the land mine?" Nancy questioned eagerly.

"Absolutely. However, it's my own opinion someone is going to be badly disappointed about this property."

"What do you mean?" Mr. Drew asked.

The surveyor lowered his voice.

"It happens I know a little about mining. After going over this property today I'm inclined to doubt that the veins of gold are very extensive. In my opinion it would cost more to mine the ore than it would ever be worth."

"Sawtice has offered my daughter a thousand dollars for the tract."

"I'd take it," the surveyor advised. "The property is of no use for farming."

"What do you think, Nancy?" her father inquired.

"I scarcely know what to say, Father. I think I'll not make my decision quite yet."

Nancy was disappointed. At first she had never dared hope that gold would be found on her land, but the events of the past few days had led her to think otherwise. It was now difficult for her to accept the truth.

"We can't stay here in the woods indefinitely," Mr. Drew told his daughter gently. "After all, the land cost you nothing, and you came here to inspect it, anticipating a possible disappointment."

"I suppose it would be best to sell, only——"

"Many a dollar has been lost because the trader held on, hoping that the market would turn."

"You're right. I'll sell. When you see Sawtice tell him I accept his offer. Only I dislike having dealings with a man of his character."

"If it turns out that he harmed Pierre Chap

in any way, there'll be another reckoning with him,'' the attorney promised.

He went to find the man, and the two conferred together for some time. Nancy joined them at her father's call.

"Mr. Sawtice has agreed to pay cash for the property,'' he informed her. "He will send a plane to the city for it immediately. As soon as the money arrives, you are to sign over the land, and we'll start home. Is that plan satisfactory?''

"Perfectly,'' Nancy declared. "Mr. Sawtice, would you object if I asked your pilot to carry a message for me to the States?''

The man frowned. He did not fancy her request, yet he could not very well refuse it.

"It's entirely up to him,'' he said gruffly. "If he wants to carry a letter, it's nothing to me.''

Before Nancy could write out a note to Annette Chapelle asking her to come North if she were able to do so, she saw Buck Sawtice talking with the airplane pilot.

"I wonder if he's telling him not to take the letter,'' she thought.

A few minutes later when she made her request to the pilot, he seemed reluctant to accommodate her.

"I don't see how I can take the note, Miss. I'll not have time to deliver it, let alone mail it anywhere.''

Raymond Niles, who was standing near by, had overheard the conversation. He was determined to make a favorable impression on Nancy, and stepped forward.

"Go ahead and take the letter," he urged the aviator. "I'll be responsible to Sawtice."

"All right," the airman agreed. "Give it to me."

Nancy handed him the message with instructions for its delivery. A little later the plane took off and was lost to view in the sky.

The girl was glad that Raymond Niles had aided her, though she did not feel especially grateful to him, for she was well aware of his purpose. She disliked the man intensely.

"Don't rush away," he coaxed her, as she turned after watching the take-off.

"I can't stop and talk now," she told him hurriedly.

She had caught a glimpse of the sheriff's possé returning from the search for Pierre Chap, and ran to meet the riders.

CHAPTER XXIII

TREACHERY

THEY regarded her coldly. Aware that something was wrong, Nancy sought the sheriff, who spoke to her in terse sentences.

"It was nothing but a hoax. We had a hard ride, only to find that no one had been imprisoned in the cave. Most likely Chap's safe in his cabin now."

"Tom Stripe probably didn't tell the truth about the hiding place, but I feel confident he knows that Pierre Chap has been imprisoned some place."

The sheriff paid slight heed to her words. He was weary from the long ride, and hoped that he might find some excuse for abandoning the entire expedition.

Nancy was mortified at the mistake she had made. Now that Pierre Chap could not be found, it would be impossible to arrest Tom Stripe. She felt discouraged at the failure of her plan.

"Surely you aren't going to abandon the search for Mr. Chap?" she queried.

"Save for the ridiculous story Tom Stripe

told you, what proof do you have that he has been kidnaped?''

''His house was boarded up, and I found a note in the oak tree.''

''The message probably was put there for a joke.''

''But it wasn't a joke that I found——''

Just in time Nancy caught herself, and refrained from divulging the discovery of the chest of money.

''Oh, go away and don't bother me,'' the sheriff said a trifle crossly.

Nancy tried to talk with some of the men and explain to them how she had made the mistake, but they did not seem to care to listen to her.

''Such an unreasonable lot,'' the girl complained later to Bess and George. ''Instead of wreaking vengeance on Tom Stripe for the trick, they let him go free, and then blame me for it all!''

Norman Ranny was equally discouraged when he returned to camp. He declared that he would set out alone and search for Pierre Chap.

''I thought when I sent for Annette that if she were to come here she might find her grandfather safe and well,'' Nancy told him. ''Now, if she should arrive to learn that he is still missing, it may prove to be a great shock to her.''

Since it was unlikely that the airplane which

Buck Sawtice had dispatched to the city would
return that evening, Nancy and her friends
made plans to camp on the site. They had
brought only the barest necessities with them,
and spent a most uncomfortable night. When
morning dawned there was still no sign of the
airplane.

Mr. Drew and his daughter were troubled at
the delay. Buck Sawtice, on the other hand,
did not seem the least bit disturbed. He kept
his men busy removing gold from the surface
vein.

"I don't like the way they're carting off my
nuggets," Nancy complained. "After all, I
haven't sold the land yet so they're really
stealing from me."

"There's nothing we can do, I am afraid,"
her father told her. "The sheriff doesn't seem
disposed to protect our interests here of late."

"I've noticed that," Nancy said ruefully.

At noon one of the sheriff's men sighted a
distant forest fire from the knoll. He reported
it to his companions, all of whom prepared to
ride away to fight it.

"Sorry we can't stay," he told Carson Drew,
"but there's nothing for us to do around here,
anyway."

"That depends upon one's viewpoint," the
attorney retorted.

Save for Norman Ranny and his friends, the
Dawsons, everyone had deserted the camp.

Buck Sawtice could not conceal his pleasure as he watched the men ride away.

"They weren't really doing us any good," Mr. Drew commented to Nancy when the two were alone, "although the psychological effect of their being here was worth while."

She nodded soberly.

"Now that the sheriff has gone, Buck Sawtice may try a few tricks."

"That's it exactly. I don't like the way he's acting."

"He seems entirely too confident about something. I can't understand why the plane hasn't returned with my money."

"Neither can I. It begins to look a trifle suspicious."

All that day the party waited. It was irritating to watch the miners at work, removing gold ore and nuggets which they chanced to find, but Nancy and her friends held their peace.

"If that plane doesn't arrive here by morning, I intend to have a show-down with Sawtice," Carson Drew told Ranny. "I'm beginning to think we've been tricked."

Nancy could not sleep that night, she was so worried about Pierre Chap. She gave little thought to her own problem, but tossed restlessly in her blankets. Finally she dressed herself and left the tent.

It was a pleasant moonlight night. Everything was quiet about the camp.

"I'll take a short walk," Nancy decided. "Perhaps that will make me tired enough to want to sleep."

She had gone but a short distance through the trees when she beheld the silhouettes of two men directly ahead of her. Creeping up closer, she heard them talking animatedly together in French.

"I'm sticking with Sawtice," she heard one of them say, "for he's a shrewd old fox. Why, I know for a fact that he never intends to pay Nancy Drew for this land. He told the airplane pilot not to bring along any money."

"So!" the other chuckled. "In a few more days we'll have most of the nuggets from the creek. Nancy Drew and her father are like two blind cats—they see nothing! Never once have they suspected Sawtice of locking the gold in a shack less than half a mile from here. Soon he will have enough, and then off we'll go to a richer field while they sit here patiently waiting for the money!"

The two men laughed heartily at the joke, and moved away. Nancy cautiously followed them, and could hear them speaking again.

"It was a good joke the way they swallowed that story Tom Stripe told them about imprisoning Pierre Chap in the cave! The sheriff's men went riding all over the country, never suspecting that Chap was secreted almost within a stone's throw of the camp!"

The conversation ran on, finally changing to a less interesting subject. Convinced that she could learn no more, Nancy returned to her tent. The walk into the woods had certainly brought her no peace of mind. Until dawn the girl lay awake, thinking and planning.

Long before her chums were awake, Nancy was abroad. She hiked a short distance upstream, and came to a high dam, which she spent the greater part of an hour inspecting. Not far away there was a shack in which dynamite was kept. A sign warned all persons to keep away. Nancy surveyed the building with interest, but did not attempt to enter it.

She returned to camp to find her father up and dressed, and immediately told him everything she had overheard. Bess and George came over to hear her story.

"I did a little exploring this morning," Nancy explained. "I thought I might find the shack where the gold nuggets are kept, but all I could see was a place where dynamite is stored."

"Why, I recall seeing an old shack not far from this camp," Bess said. "George and I were doing a little prospecting when we noticed the place. We would have investigated it, but Raymond Niles was around."

"Did he seem to be guarding the cabin?" Nancy questioned.

"Why, come to think of it, that might have

been what he was doing. He looked relieved when we walked away, didn't he, George?"

"Yes, he did. Maybe he's keeping watch over the gold nuggets!"

"Can you point out the building?" Mr. Drew asked the girls.

They assured him that they could do so.

"I have a feeling that Pierre Chap may be imprisoned near the gold shack," Nancy declared. "If we can locate the latter, we may be able to find him."

"Even if we should find the shack, it might not be easy to secure the release of Mr. Chap," Carson Drew said thoughtfully. "We are greatly outnumbered by the miners."

"And they watch our every move," George added. "Bess and I can't stir a step from camp without being followed. Nancy is spied upon the same way, too."

"I am completely disgusted with the way the sheriff failed us," Mr. Drew commented. "I dispatched word for him to return, but I have no hopes of his doing so."

"We can't afford to wait," Nancy said quietly.

"No. By delaying we will play directly into Buck Sawtice's hands. Yet I can think of no plan to outwit him."

Nancy leaned forward and lowered her voice.

"I have one," she announced.

CHAPTER XXIV

THE KEY TO THE GOLD

BUCK SAWTICE was busily writing at a table
in his tent when Nancy and her friends entered.
He looked up sharply, then offered them camp
chairs.

"Well, what is it?" he asked.

"I have come to see you about my land,"
Nancy began.

Before she could explain the proposition she
had in mind, he cut her short.

"Now don't be alarmed because the plane
hasn't returned with your money, Miss Drew.
I feel certain the pilot will arrive today."

Nancy's eyes narrowed.

"You know as well as I do he'll never bring
back the money, Mr. Sawtice. You have tried
to trick me."

The man's jaw dropped at such a bold state-
ment. He glanced quickly at Carson Drew, but
the attorney's grim expression told him more
plainly than words could that the truth had
been discovered.

"Nonsense," he denied feebly. "I am as
puzzled as you are over the delay in the deliv-

ery of the funds, though I have every confidence that the pilot will not fail me."

"He will obey orders," Nancy retorted scornfully. "I happen to know that you told him *not* to bring the money. However, I am willing to make a new deal with you."

Buck Sawtice studied her shrewdly.

"You mean you'll take less for your land?"

"I'll give it to you for nothing—on one condition."

Carson Drew sprang from his chair.

"Nancy, do you realize what you are saying?"

"Absolutely," Nancy smiled.

"What is your condition?" Sawtice asked cautiously.

"That you return Pierre Chap unharmed!"

A mask-like expression froze upon the promoter's face.

"Who is Pierre Chap?"

"You know very well who he is," Nancy countered, "for he is hidden near this camp."

"You are mistaken, Miss Drew. I am not a kidnaper."

"I am making no accusations," Nancy retorted. "However, I feel confident that if you wish to do so you can locate Pierre Chap. Should you care to accept my proposition and have him safely in camp by nightfall, I will deed over my land to the Yellow Dawn Mining Company."

"Nancy, you will lose everything by this deal," her father protested.

"I've thought it all over carefully, Father. If Mr. Sawtice accepts the proposal, I intend to go through with it."

"Suppose I should return Pierre Chap— mind I don't say that I can—what proof have I that you will keep your agreement?" Sawtice demanded.

Nancy raised up her head proudly.

"You have my word."

"And do you agree to abide by this decision of your daughter?" the promoter asked Carson Drew.

"I suppose I must, though I'll admit it goes against my grain to do so."

"What do you say?" Nancy urged.

"If your father will sign the paper as your guardian, I'll agree."

"All right, I'll sign," Carson Drew snapped. "Now are you satisfied?"

"Quite," Sawtice smiled. "I really admire your daughter for her shrewd business ability, otherwise I would decline the proposal. You know, had I wished I could have taken the land without obligating myself in any way."

Carson Drew stifled a bitter retort as he escorted the girls to the door of the tent. When the four were out of earshot of Buck Sawtice they gave vent to their pent-up feelings.

"It was nothing less than stealing," Mr.

Drew declared angrily. "Nancy, I'd never have permitted you to go through with it, had I known what you proposed to do before we went into that tent."

"That's why I didn't tell you," the girl smiled. "I lay awake last night thinking and thinking. It seemed to me the only way to save poor old Mr. Chap."

"But you'll lose everything," George wailed. "They will get all the gold."

"According to Mr. Ranny and the surveyor, the best part of it has already been taken from the land."

"But the nuggets really belonged to you," Bess maintained. "Buck Sawtice has no right to take anything until you deed the property to him. Isn't that correct, Mr. Drew?"

"Yes, it is, Bess, but up here in the woods might seems to be right."

"I wish I could save the gold, though I don't see how I can," Nancy said regretfully. "After all, Pierre Chap's life is the most important consideration. You aren't really provoked at me, are you, Father?"

The attorney squeezed her hand.

"No, I'm very proud of you, Nancy. You have been wonderfully generous. But it infuriates me to think that Sawtice is going to win out in this affair. He should be behind prison bars."

The attorney dropped his voice as Sawtice

emerged from his tent. They saw him walk across the field, and converse with several of his cronies, whereupon the four men rode out of the camp, leading an extra horse.

"They're going after Mr. Chap," Nancy was confident. "Sawtice only pretended that he didn't know where to find him."

Carson Drew left the girls to talk with Norman Ranny.

"Now is our chance to get the gold," Nancy whispered to Bess and George. "I didn't dare mention all my plans when Father was here, for he wouldn't have permitted me to attempt it."

She then outlined what she proposed to do, and Bess and George were a trifle frightened at the daring of her scheme. Yet at her insistence they were willing to attempt to carry it through.

The girls quietly slipped away from camp. Bess, who remembered where the gold shack was located, led the way. A short distance from the building they paused to talk over the situation.

"Raymond Niles is still there on guard," Bess observed.

"Then this is almost certain to be the shack where the gold is kept," Nancy said with satisfaction. "Now, girls, don't forget your parts in our little play!"

Assuming an air of innocence, the three

chums linked arms and strolled out into the clearing. Raymond Niles noticed them instantly, watching intently, but the girls pretended to be unaware of his scrutiny, and meandered toward him.

"Well, if it isn't Mr. Niles!" Nancy greeted in surprise. "I was wondering where you had been keeping yourself lately. We haven't seen you in camp much of late."

Flattered to think that his absence had been noted, the guard bestowed his best smile upon the three.

"Is this your cabin?" Bess inquired politely.

"Well, not exactly. I sort of own a part interest in it. I look after it for another fellow."

"I'd love to see the inside," Nancy said wheedlingly.

"I wish I could let you do so, but its impossible. The other fellow wouldn't like it."

"Oh," George sighed in pretended disappointment, "I did so want to peer inside. Of course, you don't mind if we just look in the window, do you?"

Before Niles was fully aware of her intention, she turned toward the window.

"Here, you mustn't do that," he cried, starting after the girl.

This was the opportunity Nancy sought. She had noticed that Niles held in his hand the key to the padlock of the door.

"Oh, please let us go inside," she pleaded, grasping him by the hand.

A foolish grin spread over the young man's face.

"I wish I could, Miss Drew, but I have to obey orders."

Nancy smiled as she quickly withdrew her hand from his. But she had the key in her possession!

"Oh, come on, girls," she called carelessly. "What do we want to see this silly old place for, anyway?"

Taking their cue, George and Bess followed her.

"Don't be in such a hurry," Niles begged. "Stay and talk a while."

They pretended not to hear him.

"Did you get the key, Nancy?" George demanded, when they were some distance away.

"I certainly did! Foolish fellow! He thinks every girl in the world is captivated by his charms."

"What do you intend to do with the key, now that you have it?" Bess inquired curiously. "If you're planning on getting that gold it won't be so easy."

"That's what I'm afraid of," Nancy admitted.

The day passed slowly. Toward night-fall men were seen coming slowly down the trail. They were leading another horse upon which

Pierre Chap was mounted. The old man slumped in the saddle and nearly collapsed when Mr. Drew and Norman Ranny hurried to assist him in alighting. They half-carried him to a nearby tent. Buck Sawtice did not give Nancy nor her father an opportunity to talk with Mr. Chap.

"I've kept my part of the agreement," he told them. "Now you must do as you promised."

The girl had the deed ready. In rapid order, scarcely pausing to read them, she signed the papers which the promoter thrust into her hand. Almost sullenly did Carson Drew add his signature to the documents.

"There, the land is yours," he said bitterly, after the final sheet had been signed. "I presume it gives you intense satisfaction to cheat my daughter out of her property!"

Back in the tent where Norman Ranny was ministering to the needs of old Mr. Chap, the Drews began to regret having kept their agreement, for they were to learn that the prisoner had been most inhumanly treated by his captors.

"They beat me nearly every day," Mr. Chap related in a cracked voice. "They tried everything they could think of to make me tell where I had hidden my money. Even after Tom Stripe learned the truth, they abused me shamefully."

"Did Buck Sawtice have anything to do with it?" Nancy demanded.

"Yes, he was the ringleader. Everything was done according to his orders. Even on the way here the men beat me."

"It was included in the agreement that Mr. Chap should be returned unharmed," Nancy said bitterly. "In every way Sawtice has broken his promises."

"If you only hadn't signed away the land!" George groaned.

"It wouldn't have been necessary had we been properly protected by the authorities," Carson Drew snapped. "We are justified in taking the law into our own hands."

"There should be some way of recovering stolen gold," Ranny declared. "If you like, I'll march into Sawtice's tent with my gun and demand a settlement."

"You would be overpowered in an instant," Nancy said. "I think I have a better plan. I've already told Bess and George about it. Wait here until we return."

The daring girls darted from the tent before they could be stopped. Racing to the gold shack, they were elated to find that Niles had left his post.

Nancy unlocked the door. With George standing guard, Nancy and Bess made a hasty search of the place. In one of the cupboards they found a heavy bag of gold nuggets.

"Quick! I think I hear someone coming!"
George warned.

Nancy and her chums grasped the precious
ore, and they ran as fast as they could back
to the tent. She thrust the heavy container
into the hand of her surprised father.

"Keep this for me! I have something more
to do!"

As she was about to dash from the tent
again, she paused to fling out some important
instructions.

"Get Mr. Chap out of here as quickly as you
can. And everyone meet me in ten minutes at
the place where our horses are tied!"

"What are you going to do?" Carson Drew
called after her.

Intent only upon her purpose, Nancy did not
hear him. She ran up the path which led to
the dynamite shack. It was her plan to change
the course of the stream by blasting the power
dam.

"It's a risky thing to attempt," she told herself grimly, "but if I succeed, Sawtice will
never be able to use my property!"

CHAPTER XXV

RUSHING WATERS

NANCY reached the shack, and was elated to find it unlocked. She carefully selected a large stick of dynamite from among the stores of explosives, and carried it gingerly to the dam.

Balancing herself dexterously, she moved far out upon the structure, and placed the charge so that it would explode in the most advantageous place. She hesitated but an instant, and then struck a match, which she applied to the long fuse. The flame began to eat its way slowly toward the stick.

Pausing only long enough to make certain that the fire would not go out, Nancy turned and fled. She was all out of breath when she reached her friends.

"Mount, and ride for your lives!" she cried.

Carson Drew slung the heavy nugget bag over the saddle of his horse. Norman Ranny rode double, supporting Pierre Chap. They all raced for the knoll. Even before they reached it, there came a terrific blast!

"What was that?" Mr. Drew shouted, drawing rein.

"Don't stop now!" Nancy cried, striking at

the flank of his horse. "Ride on! Ride on!"

They reached the hillock in safety. Then Nancy pointed with a trembling hand to the torrent of water that was flooding down the valley, and coursing over the ground they had recently left.

"You dynamited the dam!" her father exclaimed.

"Yes, for that was the only way I could prevent Sawtice from using my property. Now it will be covered with several feet of water. The mining tools and equipment will be destroyed, but I warned the workers to stay away from the valley."

Fascinated, the party stood upon the high ground and watched the water as it spread out over the land. The erstwhile camp soon became a lake.

"I'm glad Sawtice and his men escaped," Nancy said soberly, "even though they are scoundrels."

After Mr. Chap's story had been told to the authorities, warrants were issued for the arrest of Buck Sawtice and his fellow conspirators. Tom Stripe and Raymond Niles were apprehended almost immediately, though several days passed before Sawtice was placed behind jail bars. He was scheduled to be tried for participation in many fraudulent schemes.

Shortly after Nancy and her friends returned to Wellington Lake, Annette Chap arrived by airplane in response to the urgent message she had received. She had recovered rapidly from her accident, and looked almost as well as she had the day she first met Nancy.

"I'm not very strong yet," the writer confessed ruefully. "But I know I shall feel better after I've spent a few weeks at the old homestead. Grandfather Pierre and I intend to get well together."

When Nancy saw the two of them, happy at being reunited, she never once regretted signing away her land. Of course, most of the valuable nuggets had been removed before the property was flooded. Yet had all the gold been lost, she would not have wanted things to turn out otherwise. Mrs. Donnelly insisted that Norman Ranny remain at her home with the others, for a reconciliation had been effected between the Ranny and Donnelly families, due to Nancy's efforts.

In tracing down the unscrupulous practices of the Yellow Dawn Company, it was definitely proven that Tom Stripe had caused most of the trouble between the two women. He, too, had forged the document which had been received by the Velvet Company, and had sold considerable worthless stock. Both Mrs. Donnelly and Mrs. Ranny were overjoyed to learn that some of the money they had lost in securities would eventually be returned to them.

"Speaking of money, I never dreamed that

I was holding a small fortune in my hands when Nancy gave me that bag of gold," Mr. Drew ruminated, as they were all seated before the crackling fire in Mrs. Donnelly's sitting room. He chuckled softly to himself. "I guess it isn't the first time I've been left holding the bag!"

"How much do you suppose the gold will be worth?" Nancy queried.

"A very tidy sum," Norman Ranny told her. "Far more than your land would ever have brought you."

"I'll send it to the assayer's for you," Mr. Drew promised. "How do you want it? In gold coins, or one huge bar?"

"I think gold coins would be more useful," Nancy said gaily.

Pierre Chap had looked highly distressed at the mention of money. When Nancy asked him what the trouble was he confessed to the group that his entire fortune had been stolen by Tom Stripe.

"I had intended that Annette should have the money," he said sadly. "That scoundrel forced me to tell him where I had hidden the chest. Now, even though he has been caught, I doubt if I will ever get back any of it."

"Why, Mr. Ranny and I dug up your chest "and re-buried it," Nancy informed him. "Everything happened so rapidly that I completely forgot to mention it to you."

After a day of rest Nancy and her chums returned to the Chap homestead with the prospector, Annette, and her grandfather. They found the chest where it had been hidden, not far from the ancient oak tree.

Before the girls returned to join Carson Drew at Wellington Lake where he was still busy gathering data concerning the Taylor lumber case, Annette Chap drew them aside for a little confession.

"Norman and I are to be married next week. We feel that we have waited too long as it is," she said.

"I am so glad," Nancy beamed. "I hope that I've perhaps had a tiny part in your happiness."

"You've been the whole cause of it," the novelist assured her gratefully. "As long as I live I shall never forget your kindness to me. Not only did you reunite Norman and myself, but you saved Grandfather from a dire fate."

"I think the hollow oak did it all," Nancy smiled. "If it hadn't been for the message left inside it, I can't imagine how things might have terminated."

"Speaking of the hollow oak reminds me of another thing I have to tell you," the woman smiled. "Norman and I plan to build our new home on this very site."

"Near the oak tree?"

"Yes, for we've grown greatly attached to

it. Besides, the property will be near Grandfather Pierre's cabin.''

''Don't you feel sad to think of giving up your career as a writer and coming back home to live?'' Nancy asked presently.

Annette shook her head.

''I'd gladly give it up, if need be. However, this is an ideal place in which to write. Although I shall have to relinquish my movie contracts, there will be more time for me to write thought-provoking novels.''

''I am sure you will be very happy here,'' Nancy said, smiling.

When Nancy and her friends returned to Lake Wellington they found that Carson Drew had completed all his business matters, and was eager to start back for the United States.

Before they left the North Woods the girls inquired about the condition of their former guide, Pete Atkins. Great was their relief to learn that he was well on the road to recovery.

''I wish you didn't need to hurry away,'' Mrs. Donnelly protested, as she bade good-bye to her young charges.

''So do we,'' Bess and George told her in unison.

''We'll try to come back next summer, if you care to have us,'' Nancy declared. ''But you must promise not to provide us with so much excitement.''

Mrs. Donnelly laughed heartily.

"I think the only way I could promise that would be for me to keep all of you locked up in one room!"

As they were en route to River Heights, Carson Drew disclosed that the trip north had been a highly successful one for him.

"I have absolute proof now that Buck Sawtice is involved dishonorably in the Marcus Taylor lumber matter," he told the girls. "If I don't win that case now I'm not worth much as a lawyer."

When the train pulled into River Heights, Nancy was amazed to see that almost everyone in town had turned out to welcome home the little group. Hannah Gruen was the first one to greet the girl as she stepped from the platform.

"My! My! If it isn't good to have you home again," she cried, wiping a tear from her eye. "It seems as if you've been gone a year."

Nancy smiled in appreciation. "I must admit it was one of the most exciting vacations of my life!"

At the time she did not realize that soon she was to become involved in an adventure just as thrilling, to be called by her chums "The Mystery of the Ivory Charm."

"Did you bring the bag of gold with you?" the housekeeper whispered anxiously.

Nancy laughed gleefully.

"No, I'm thankful to say that Father has relieved me of that responsibility. The gold is at the assayer's now. I won't know for several weeks how much coin I am to receive for it."

Shortly after the Drews returned to River Heights, the Marcus Taylor case came up for trial. No one was surprised to learn that the lumberman had been awarded a large sum in damages, for Carson Drew had gathered such a vast array of evidence that no other verdict would have been possible.

One day Nancy received a long letter from Annette Chap. The young woman enclosed a photograph of the famous old oak on the Chap property. Nancy placed it carefully away in a drawer that held some of her choicest possessions.

The letter contained considerable news. Buck Sawtice had been brought to trial. He had been convicted on many counts, and sent to prison for a long term. Tom Stripe and Raymond Niles had escaped with lighter sentences.

After discussing the events Nancy seated herself upon the arm of her father's chair, and playfully tweaked his ear. "As my legal adviser, how would you suggest that I spend my gold?" she asked.

Carson Drew thoughtfully blew several smoke rings to the ceiling before answering. His eyes twinkled as he replied:

"I was just thinking that you might want to buy a little real estate."

Nancy glanced ruefully at her father to see if he really was serious. Then she laughed heartily.

"Father, if anyone should ever offer me another deed, I'd run a mile!" she said. "After having had so many exciting adventures up North, I think I'll agree to your holding title to all the property that comes into the Drew family!"

THE END